TRUSSED

The MASTERED Saga, Book 2

K.L. Silver

*TRUSSED: To tie or secure (the body) closely or tightly; bind (often followed by up).

*TRUST: A firm belief in the reliability, truth, ability, or strength of someone or something.

Copyright © 2015 K.L. Silver

ISBN: 978-1-928121-17-6
Published by K.L. Silver

Dedication

To my children: Marli, Matthew, Cassandra, Tiger and Roxanna. Whether they like it or not.

Acknowledgments

There is no 'I' in NOVEL. It takes a lot of support and technical know-how to so-called self-publish a book. I'm grateful for the fine folks that have held my hand and helped me up along the way.

Alexandra Lucas has been instrumental in so many ways, I can't begin to list them. It would be a novel unto itself.

Nancy Pracht is my PA, heads up my street team, and makes me laugh every day. (And cry). This woman is ALWAYS up!

My beautiful Belles (Silver's Ballsy Belles) make up the ballsiest street team in town. I appreciate each and every one of you!

Dee and Ell are both creative, talented, and generous. Wow, just wow!

Last but not least, a special shout-out to Michael, a Ballsy Belle, a wonderful friend, and a great sounding board!

SPANK YOU ALL!

Prologue

Missy teetered precariously on the soft edge between slumber and wakefulness. She reveled in the weight of him, snoring softly atop her. She had one last conscious thought before succumbing completely.

She contemplated what might be required in order to merit her collar back. She knew in her heart that whatever the task, she would perform it with the utmost of pride.

He was her Master. She would never doubt him again.

With cum-stained lips curled into a contented half-smile of anticipation, Missy joined James in deep, dreamless sleep...

Chapter 1

The acrid stench of sweat and sex hung in the air, unmistakable. Missy's nostrils twitched in recognition of the subtler, underlying scents, most notably her Master's cigar and his favorite cologne. All were long stale, not that it made a whiff of difference. If James didn't shower for a month, it would be her pleasure to lick him clean from head to toe, and, of course—everywhere in between. She wouldn't forget to thank him for the privilege, either.

Submissive…

She knew where she was long before full consciousness dawned to confirm it. At last, she was where she'd always belonged: in her Master's bed. She lay motionless, basking in the moment and luxuriating in the distinctive notes of his essence.

The pheromones the man excreted so casually ought to come with a warning label. They were as entrancing as a hypnotist, as addictive as top grade heroin. The past few months were proof positive that Missy's 'habit' was impossible to break. With shameless abandon, she gave up and gave in.

As far as she was concerned, quitting was for quitters, and she was no quitter. James was her drug of choice and she was blissfully hooked. The only things missing were the tourniquet and sunken, track-marked veins.

She felt surprisingly rested, considering the harrowing events of the previous night. After years of harassment and two futile police reports, her deadbeat ex-husband had finally crossed the line. While her nerves were a little worse for wear as a result, there was also a sense of elation. Overall, she'd emerged unscathed.

Missy knew how lucky she was. She also knew that she owed it all, and only, to James. Without a doubt, the outcome would have been much different had he not arrived when he did. Missy frowned, disallowing unpleasant memories from the night before to disturb her serenity.

As if on cue, the seductive aroma of fresh brewed coffee interrupted her musings. Her mouth watered a la Pavlov's dog post dinner bell. Her belly grumbled, making its dissatisfied presence heard.

Missy couldn't help but smile. The dried semen that coated her cheeks pulled back in resistance. It was that crude stimulus that triggered more agreeable memories from the previous evening. The terror of Luke's attempted assault paled in comparison to the joy of kneeling on the cold hardwood floor of James' foyer. It was there she'd sucked his cock until he'd spurted gobs of cum into her face. 'Good girl' may well be the two sexiest words she'd ever heard.

Master...

Even as she blushed, her smile widened. Stretched to the breaking point, the crusted ejaculate finally gave, cracking in uneven patches before flaking away. The simple truth was that in James' presence, her cocoon of protective layers became redundant, an unnecessary burden. With James, Missy was free to be Missy: the good, the bad, and yes—the submissive.

She wasn't bad, she was submissive, and it felt so good. Where her feelings of being 'different' used to frighten and confuse, she now felt pride. Her angst-inducing lack of interest in the opposite sex now made perfect sense. Her 'nasty' fantasies of rough anal sex no longer horrified. James accepted her for who and what she was, without judgment and without reservation.

A fantasy come true, until I screwed it up!

Yet, just when she'd lost all hope of reconciliation, he arrived in the nick of time, saving her from from the evil villain – *and* from herself. Grinning, Missy decided their love story would make an epic novel.

She was eager to begin the first page of the rest of their lives. Opening her eyes in anticipation of doing just that, blackness greeted her. Mystified, her heart rate spiked as it dawned on her that she was blindfolded. While the material was soft as gossamer, nary a single ray of light penetrated.

Her mind, which until now had been tripping the light fantastic, snapped to full alertness. She moved instinctively to eradicate the unsettling sensation.

This, too, proved impossible.

Missy was stunned to find herself not only blindfolded, but restrained—wrists and ankles trussed to the four corners of James' bed. In her mind's eye, she envisioned the sturdy inlaid columns and understood that resistance was futile.

Bound naked, her breathing escalated, her ears rang, and last but far from least—her pussy gushed.

Whore!

Yes, at long last she was exactly where she belonged. It would appear she wasn't leaving any time soon...

Chapter 2

Even as she began to struggle instinctively against the binds, Missy was aware of her exposed labia thickening and her clitoris distending with blatant desire. There was no misinterpreting her body's raw, unsolicited response to the defenseless position in which she found herself.

She shook her head, bewildered by the tangible confirmation of her deviant nature. Her chance encounter with the captivating James Colton had unlocked something deep within her. She'd been forced to examine a part of herself she'd long shunned.

There'd been nothing for her to do but acknowledge the truth.

Submissive...

She'd always known there was something 'wrong' with her. Worse, polite society would be quick to agree. She'd quaked in her self-imposed closet, tried hard to be 'normal'. Too hard. The battle had begun to wear on her, stress and anxiety her closest companions.

That all ended the moment she and James locked eyes that fateful day at the grocery store. In that instant, life as she knew it was forever changed.

An image of Mr. Spock's Vulcan mind meld floated before her veiled eyes. Missy would have giggled, given different circumstances. As it was, every hair on her body rose up in unison from their respective follicles, probing.

Not for escape, mind you. No, Missy's body had but one objective and that was to locate James.

Master...

She called out his name, softly at first, then louder. Other than her stuttered breathing, silence prevailed. Yet, his presence encompassed her, permeated her. She could almost see him through eyes incapable of sight.

Where is he? Her ears strained, struggling to compensate for the lost sense. Still nothing. She felt alone, bound in blackness, and nearly frantic for James. After what seemed an eternity, she began to squirm in earnest.

Accomplishing nothing, her mind snapped to the strange, complex series of knots that James used to subdue Luke the night before. She pictured the astonished faces of the two responding police officers. Upon closer examination of the knotted nylons, their aloof, seen-it-all demeanor changed to one of deference.

If James had given them a direct order, Missy wouldn't have been surprised if they'd obeyed. In truth, she'd have been more surprised if they hadn't. Recognizing her struggle as a pointless waste of energy, she stopped her fretting and settled into the binds.

I'll be released when my Master is good and ready, and not a moment before...

She took comfort in the knowledge that she was precisely where James desired. Her trust in him was eternal, her need for him a steady stream between her legs. Missy had nowhere to go and all the time in the world to get there. Her ragged breathing slowed and she closed her unseeing eyes.

Splayed wide and bound tight, she fell into a deep, peaceful sleep...

Chapter 3

James Colton observed every intake of breath, every twitch, every contraction. He drank her in as intently as a lion partook of a swollen stream after a long drought. He was only too aware of how close he'd come to losing her. He was not ashamed to admit that it terrified him.

He flinched, imagining the scene he'd have come upon had he arrived at her home just seconds later. With military precision, he relived every detail of the previous evening.

He remembered tearing her drunken, two-hundred and forty pound ex-husband off of her as though he weighed nothing. The motherfucker already had his grimy pants unzipped, although James doubted the drug-addled lush had attained any semblance of an erection in years.

Nonetheless, even without actually raping her, Luke had done more than enough damage. Emotional angst aside, there were bruises on her chest where he'd shoved her and on her thighs where the fat fucker pinned her.

A single, leftover bolt of adrenaline from the night before shot through him. Time slowed while his mind raced. His military training kicked in as though he were back in the oilfields of Kuwait, every sense tingling.

It took some willpower to unclench his fists. Consciously slowing his pulse, he reminded himself to check on the status of Lukie-boy's pathetic ass. James wanted the book thrown at him – hard! He intended to do everything in his power to ensure that happened. He had the names and numbers of the two cops on the scene, not to mention his good friend, The Honorable George T. Weatherly, magistrate.

In this case, James was not above using whatever, or whomever, was at his disposal to see his objectives met. Losing Missy, either by his own pigheaded stupidity or by Luke's cowardly hand, would be no less agonizing than amputating a vital part of his physical being. An arm. A leg.

A heart...

James had to admit that he relished the task of expunging the entire ordeal from her mind, if only for a short time. The thought caused his tumescent cock to twitch in sweet anticipation. He wouldn't have long to wait.

Entrenched in a cozy armchair wearing a cozy pair of low-slung pajama bottoms, James observed as she struggled against the silken restraints. His gaze shifted from one bind to the next, inspecting the integrity of each. He wasn't surprised to find them pristine. His eyes settled on the framed photo of Missy on the bedside table. Beside that sat the collar that belonged around her neck.

Submissive...

Fuck, she's beautiful! Still, her beauty transcended what a camera could capture. It emanated from her very soul. Remembering their delicious, and lascivious, evening at Dominic's Crab Shack, James smiled. He was sure their waiter recalled the occasion with great fondness, as well. *Every time he whacked off!*

Chuckling to himself, James reached for the mug of coffee at his elbow and took a cautious sip. In his caffeine-addicted opinion, it was one thing to inflict a little pain in the pursuit of heightened pleasure. Yet, a day without java was just plain cruel.

There were only two civilized ways to begin the day. Coffee was one. He didn't bother to suppress the wolfish smirk that the second evoked.

He was less than three feet away from Missy's naked and writing body. She couldn't catch a cold and him not see it coming. She was most fetching bound to his bed, he noted. The binds were symbolic, and he intended to make his point crystal clear. The last time they'd spent the night together, he'd woken to find her AWOL, the collar he'd bestowed upon her unlocked and abandoned.

She had much to atone for and much to learn. Judging from her swamp of a pussy, she was going to enjoy the arduous process as much as he was.

Whore!

Quite frankly, he could sit here and look at her until the end of time. Missy was to his heart what oxygen was to his lungs. After losing his wife to a freak asthma attack three years ago, he fully expected to spend the rest of his life alone, mired in guilt and remorse.

To his Dominant way of thinking, he'd failed Angeline when she needed him most. There'd been no hope of absolution. He'd been more than her husband, he'd been her Master. She should have been safest in his arms.

Instead, she'd died in them.

Yet, three years later when he'd laid eyes on Missy, it was as though life were just beginning. The level on which they connected was unprecedented for both of them. Words were unnecessary. Hearts communed and souls entwined. He was born to Master her as she was born to submit to him. Each was born to love and cherish the other. It was just that simple.

Feeling the luckiest of men, James drank in the delectable sight before him. Missy was exactly where she belonged—in his bed, well and properly trussed.

He meant to keep her as such...

Chapter 4

Beautifully bound, the silken tethers suited Missy to a T.

On the other hand, the blindfold had been an arduous decision for James. It deprived him of witnessing the surprise in her magnificent eyes when she awoke to find herself at his mercy. While it was crucial to creating the initial ambiance, he regretted it, nonetheless. He smirked. They would both be relieved of it shortly.

What little was visible above the blindfold could only be described as an unbridled mess. Missy's locks were everywhere: spread kinked and curled and chaotic across and around and under the pillow. Luke had made his clumsy and destructive entrance just as Missy was exiting the shower. The distressed tresses spoke to the harrowing experience she'd endured.

James, however, saw only beauty and bravery in every tangled strand. He was taken aback when his cock expanded along with his heart at the idea of taking a brush to the auburn curls. He envisioned her on her knees between his legs, enjoying her Master's ministrations. Pre-cum began to seep through the light cotton fabric of his pajama bottoms.

Patience, James, patience...

Indisputably, spread-eagled never looked so good. He followed the sleek lines of her body, stretched and open for his viewing pleasure. Flat on her back with her arms overhead, the outline of her ribcage was sharply accentuated. From there, her belly became a concave hollow, hip bones jutting in dramatic contrast.

She's lost weight...

Sighing, he knew precisely where to lay blame. It was a badge of dishonor he was not proud to wear. He had caused, and prolonged, the unnecessary suffering of the woman he adored. As a Dominant, he held himself to a higher standard. His behavior had been no better than that of a scorned and petulant juvenile.

He vowed to do better. He would have his whore with some meat on her bones, and in very short order at that.

Now...where was I?

Her exquisite breasts beckoned, not too big and not too small. They sat saucily atop her chest, undulating and quivering with the smallest movement. James kept the temperature down, as evidenced by the goose bumps that dimpled her flesh and tautened her over-sized nipples.

There was no doubt those sensitive peaks would enchant him until the end of time. Missy's beauty came from within, requiring little external enhancement. It shone with an intensity so dazzling, he was blinded to such gravitational mundanities as wrinkles and sagging breasts.

Time was something that could run out in a heartbeat. He'd learned that the hard way.

Adjusting his cock, James drank in the long, well-defined legs right up until they met the sensual flare of her hips. There, his attention was diverted by that which lay between.

That's enough!

Patience depleted, he picked up the fly swatter and advanced on the irresistible morsel bound helpless to his bed.

"Good morning, my precious. I trust you slept well?"

Without pausing for a response, he snapped the fly swatter against one tender nipple. Dead-on accurate, Missy's reaction was immediate, not to mention well worth the wait.

Her back arched and her tits jiggled. At the same time, her mouth opened, no doubt to emit a well-justified scream. Before it could escape, James smothered her lips with his own. The scream was lost in the intensity of the kiss, replaced instead with a long, guttural moan.

Missy's head lifted from the pillow as their tongues came together and their souls reunited. His hand cupped her face ever-so-gently, belying the vicious swat of just moments ago. Her arms jerked uselessly against their tethers in their need to draw him closer. When he slid the tips of two fingers the length of her gaping slit, he knew her inability to touch him served only to wet her further.

Pulling back, James spoke against her seeking lips.

"Have you forgotten your manners, little one? I didn't hear you thank me..."

Chapter 5

THWACK!

Missy twisted this way, then that. Her eyes welled with tears and her body was slick with sweat. There was no escaping the blows. Randomly timed but precisely placed, they rained down on both juddering breasts. Each distended nipple was allotted equal attention.

SNAP!

She couldn't place the offending instrument, but she could certainly vouch for its veracity. Her breasts were on fire, the flames radiating into her soul, her psyche, and most disconcerting—between her legs. Blatant desire flowed unabated, reminiscent of molten lava.

SWAT!

To make matters worse, between each blow James took the offended nubbin between his lips and suckled it with a tenderness that caused her breath to catch and her heart to melt.

CRACK!

Yes, the burn was intense but so was the yearn. Missy lost track at number nine, when pleasure and pain came together—and so did she. Teeth gritted, her breath escaped in ragged bursts. Much like her orgasm, which squirted out from between her legs with a force that was shocking.

Whore!

Horrified at her wanton display, she hid in the dark behind the blindfold. With all logical thought discombobulated, she played the ostrich. Missy pretended that if she couldn't see James, James couldn't see her—nor her shameless response to his harsh ministrations.

Of course, that was absurd.

"Well, well, well. I see my greedy little whore has difficulty discerning reward from punishment. Rest assured, pet, that any mercy I exhibit this morning is a direct result of the nightmare you endured last night."

Despite her acute discomfiture, Missy's heart filled to overflowing for this exceptional man. Combining pain with pleasure, tenderness with tyranny, and understanding with obstinacy, he triggered innate responses that left her weak, wanting, and most telling of all— wet.

Master...

James exacted his pound of flesh in the most captivating of ways. More often than not, she was left wishing he'd taken two. She could attest to the fact that he was a stern taskmaster. His expectations were indeed high. But, so too was her deep-rooted, hard-wired desire to meet – no, *exceed* them.

He'd shone a light into the darkest, dankest corners of her being and loved her not *in spite* of what he discovered, but because of it. Disregarding the multiple 'Do Not Enter' signs, he'd swung open a door she'd kept triple-bolted for a lifetime. Out from behind it tumbled one terrifying, socially-repugnant word.

Submissive...

The damning word fit like it was created with her in mind. At long last, she realized what had kept her from exploring this vital piece of herself. It wasn't so much the harsh truth. After all, a lifetime of debaucherous fantasies left little doubt as to her unnatural 'tendencies'.

No, her fears were more to do with another, even less appealing word: Deviant. Missy had no desire to be found out, labeled, and ostracized from the only world she'd ever known.

The truth was that before James, she'd merely existed, a square peg in the circular fabric of society. She'd avoided self-analysis like the plague. Her reclusive life revolved around paying the mortgage and her one source of joy— Christopher.

Yet, with just a glance, one kindred spirit recognized the other, melding them together for all eternity. Safe in James' embrace, Missy discovered a whole new world: the dark and delicious world of Dominance and submission. There, her mind found peace and her spirit soared.

In the blink of an eye, the jig was up. There could be no further denial of the clear-cut facts. James was the man of her dreams and of her fantasies. It was time to let the chips fall where they may.

Missy sighed, calm and content...

Chapter 6

"Mind you, I wouldn't become too complacent if I were you, my precious. Considering the impudence that brought us to this juncture, we both know you have much to make up for. As a gentleman and a Dominant, I plan on giving you every opportunity."

His words almost danced, snapping Missy out of her reverie. She could well imagine the corners of his sensuous mouth lifting. The devilish grin was inherent in every syllable.

James emphasized his statement with the tool he was using to chastise her—whipping it through the air until it hummed. The ominous effect sent an army of shivers marching up Missy's spine. They didn't let up till they'd reached her scalp.

Just then, without word or warning, he brought the infuriating instrument down for one final, emphatic strike.

WHHHAP!

With precise intent, both swollen nipples were spared. Her fat, throbbing clit, however, was not.

It took a soundless, surreal moment for the impact to sink in. Once it did, Missy all but levitated from the bed. Howling like a banshee, blood roared in her ears as all remnants of her powerful orgasm were wiped away with the single merciless wallop.

Missy's world behind the blindfold went from bottomless black to blazing white. Devoid of breath, she could only whimper, her focus narrowed to a size of a pinprick. Unaware that her arms were free of their binds, they wound around James' neck of their own accord. His mouth devoured hers, demanding her tongue even as it was proffered.

Missy's head spun. Just yesterday, both James and his king-size, four-poster bed seemed well beyond her reach. That it was nobody's fault but her own had only made it worse. She'd relived her fateful decision on that regrettable morning more times than she cared to count.

The idea that she so cavalierly tossed away his collar, the most symbolic of endowments, was almost impossible to wrap her head around.

What was I thinking?

The complete and unabridged litany of 'if onlys' cued in her head. How she longed to feel the bulky adornment locked snug around her throat once again. One thing was certain. She would never make that mistake twice!

Missy kissed him back with a passion so all-consuming, it brought tears to her eyes...

Chapter 7

James' cock strained, well past the point of patience. Even the roomy pajama bottoms had their limits, and his distended dick seemed intent on pushing them. The 'tent' it created was comical. It looked as though it could sleep six!

Even as he chuckled at his clever word play, the waffled pattern on Missy's swollen tits drew his attention. Cherry red and mottled, the fly swatter's unique imprint was quite fetching against the flawless alabaster of her skin. As she vibrated from his final, well-placed blow, her full breasts joggled for his viewing pleasure.

He used both hands to spread her sopping pussy lips. Bending close enough for her to feel his breath hot on her already steaming hole, he examined the remainder of his handiwork. Amidst a breathless concerto of dainty gasps and unladylike grunts, James congratulated himself on his choice of utensil.

Missy's entire pubis was inflamed, her clit a bloated, pulsating crimson. It didn't surprise him that her convulsing sex oozed shamelessly, just further evidence of her wanton nature. The sheets between her legs were soaked.

In wordless appreciation, he applied pressure to the slippery labia lips pulled wide between his fingertips. In short order, a frantic squeal escaped her lips.

"Did you say something, my darling? Hmmm...?"

James snorted, cracking himself up. After all, Missy's ability to communicate was greatly curtailed at the moment. Its use expended, the fly swatter's flexible plastic shaft was now ensconced between her bared teeth. She couldn't have answer if she wanted to. He added the polite suggestion that she *not* drop it.

Missy nodded furiously, making further 'discussion' unnecessary. The point was moot. Instructions were issued and there was no doubt they'd be followed to the letter.

Submissive...

Saliva seeped unchecked from between her clenched teeth. It dribbled down her chin, winding up in an ever-expanding pool in the hollow where her collar bones met. He patted her on the head as he might a puppy with a bone.

"Good girl!"

Drawing his jutting cock from the overextended bottoms, he fed it inch by inch into her sodden, grasping cunt. Once buried to the hilt, James fucked her hard, their hip bones grinding. He grunted into her obstructed mouth with each powerful stroke and she grunted back with the impact. With his girth stretching her to the limit, he bottomed out with each downward plunge. The fact that it was their first time having vaginal sex did not escape.

He glanced up and their eyes locked. Hers were the size of saucers, loving and luminous. Their ethereal beauty tugged at his heart even as a fresh surge of blood caused his balls to tighten and his cock to jerk meaningfully.

On the edge, James took hold of both bobbling nipples and held on tight. He looked past the mess of smudged mascara and crusted ejaculate straight to the core of her soft, submissive soul. If pressed, he'd swear it opened for his perusal, imploring him to uncover long-buried secrets meant only for his eyes.

Sawing into her, the walls of her tight cunt milked his cock. Deep pelvic muscles contracted with every up-stroke, begging him to stay. And to come!

Groaning, James increased his pace. A huge load was churning in his balls, moments away from delivery. Their eyes melted into each others. Missy's pupils were dilated. More spittle ran down her chin with every short, rasping breath. Nothing existed other than their straining bodies and communing minds.

With only her bullet hard nipples for balance, James threw back his head and howled. It sounded like an entire pack of wolves at the peak of breeding season. His sperm sluiced into her in one mind blowing, unending gush, cock hard as concrete. His ballsac convulsed, squeezing out every last drop.

It was at that moment that her lips parted, her primal wail uncontainable as she bucked against him in the throes of a second soul-searing orgasm.

The fly swatter landed on the pillow beside her head...

Chapter 8

Smiling like a loon, Missy luxuriated in the Jacuzzi bath.

James had filled the oval tub to the brim, then turned the countless jets to 'HIGH'. She'd giggled when the once-placid water erupted into a roiling ocean of white-capped waves. Her world was clouded with a mist of fine spray.

He'd lifted her trembling body from his bed and carried her like a baby to the ensuite bath. Having his muscular arms around her was a feeling so exquisite, it was indescribable. There was no door between the Master's chamber and his bath, nothing to impede his progress – or to provide privacy.

She remembered his ominous words from months ago. He'd been perfectly clear, letting her know that if her 'decision' was yes, her future would be "devoid of secrets and privacy".

"I will know all—the woman, the person, the whore. I will be fluent in your fears and your fantasies. I will have full knowledge of every hope, every limit, every dream. I shall gorge on your deference and delight in your surrender!"

Despite the warmth of the swirling water, Missy shivered. Despite the shivers, her pulse raced and her clit thickened. It was as though a lifetime of ambivalence towards the opposite sex had culminated in an unquenchable craving for this one man.

Submissive...

Leaning back against the curved ledge of the tub, she took several cleansing breaths. On the inhalations, she smelled bacon, and her mouth watered. She hadn't eaten in almost eighteen hours. *If you could call that eating.* She felt so sick after seeing James with another woman, she hardly touched her dinner.

Unbidden, the humiliating scene at The Pitts came to mind. She could almost taste the sour bile that flooded her throat after getting an eyeful of that...that *creature* that clung to James like a cancer.

Certain that all hope had been lost, her despair had known no bounds. As soon as the coast was clear, she'd bolted from the restaurant. Missy winced, recalling how the taxi made it to the curb just in time. She'd barely managed to get the door open before throwing up what little she'd ingested.

Humiliation aside, she acknowledged a niggling pang of guilt over Ethan Montgomery III. Due to insurmountable obstacles, she'd cut out on him not once, but twice now.

I probably shouldn't have fucked him either.

She sighed. At the time, it seemed the best hope of exorcising James. She'd hoped to get back to the half-life she'd half-lived before he'd turned it totally upside down. Instead, it served only as sad confirmation that there *was* no going back. The future that had yawned before her looked as bleak as her past. Once James Colton entered her life, all other avenues were lost to her. Every road led straight back to him.

Master...

Missy determined to call Ethan and apologize. He had good reason to be pissed. On the other hand, there was a strong possibility that her bad behavior didn't raise a single blip on his radar. After all, if he were the eligible bachelor-slash-wealthy financier-slash-woman magnet that he proclaimed, he should already have a hot date lined up.

In fact, she hoped so!

Missy stretched in the oversized tub, feeling aches in places she didn't know existed. Traumatic memories from Luke's attack wrestled for a foothold in her mind, but she wrestled them back, refusing them traction. She would not allow Luke to ruin her life for a second time. He would get his well-deserved comeuppance and she could get on with her well-deserved life.

The whirlpool jets massaged her, currents colliding willy-nilly. Licking wayward droplets from her lips, she tasted her Master's seed, and licked again. She'd been surprised when he pulled out just when she'd started to cum, leaving her twanging pussy to grasp at nothing but air. Instead, he'd stuffed his sopping member into her mouth, causing her nostrils to flare in a frantic search for oxygen.

The tang of her own juices was unexpected on her tongue. She'd pulled back, grimacing.

The sting came just as she caught the flash of his hand from the corner of her eye. James didn't slap her hard enough to cause pain, just hard enough to get her undivided attention. The fact that it caused her infuriating pussy to ooze as well spoke volumes. Missy shook her head in wonder.

Whore!

"Clean your Master's cock, whore, no hands. And get that look of distaste off your face!"

Missy looked up. Way up. Past washboard abs and cobra lats. Past broad shoulders and jutting delts. She looked straight up into the rugged face of the man she adored. She slurped on his viscous member with gusto, focusing on the task at hand and the warm approval that radiated from his eyes.

Ensconced in her Master's bath with her marked breasts bobbling atop the frothy waves, Missy recalled how he'd dislodged strands of cum-matted hair from her sticky lips. Ever-so-gently, he'd tucked them behind her ear and out of the way. At the same time, he'd pressed his cock deep into her throat. The incongruity of his actions had held her spellbound and leaking in equal proportion.

Considering her mouth was otherwise engaged, she'd done her best to convey her feelings through her efforts and her eyes.

His next words might have shook her to the core if she weren't already convinced that he could read her mind.

"Yes, little one. Master loves his precious whore!"

Chapter 9

She was late. Again...

"Dah-link! Shall I dock you twenty minutes just like old times? Hmmm...?"

Teresa's shrill voice and over-the-top fabricated accent all but demanded that heads turn and tongues wag. The psychedelic Gucci scarf she wore wrapped around her mountain of frizzled hair was a conversation unto itself. Missy's ex-boss squeezed her with the fierceness of a mama bear before holding her at arm's length for a thorough head-to-toe.

Missy was well aware that the little sundress hung on her gaunt frame. The months of separation from James weren't exactly conducive to working up an appetite.

He'd taken her home to retrieve her car and a few personal belongings. He'd insisted she stay with him for a few days, at least. She'd done her best to convince him she was well enough to meet the girls, but had fallen short. He knew better. The dark shadow of doubt remained in his eyes, a random tic played at his jaw.

Missy resisted the urge to press her lips against that tic, to lap at it with her tongue, to whisper sweet words against it. She was running late and still needed to find something to wear that would cover the purple bruises on her knees.

His concern touched her, moved her to the brink of tears. It wasn't borne of pettiness or insecurity. The sense of responsibility he felt for her was as palpable as his love. Her submissive heart skipped a beat. She'd promised to not be late. Again.

"I can't believe these words are about to come out of my mouth, but, you're too skinny, little Miss Missy!"

Her ex-boss's words cut through her reverie like a designer's needle through silk. She was a firm believer that one could never be too skinny, nor too rich. For her to find anyone 'too' skinny was unheard of.

"Look who's talking!" Missy shot back, hugging Teresa again before moving on to Stephanie. She was waiting with open arms, an ear to ear grin on her sweet, familiar face. Missy was fond of both of these women, having worked shoulder to shoulder with them for over seven years.

Deciding to lunch poolside, they started with sparkling water with lime wedges. It wasn't long before they graduated to tequila shooters with lemon wedges. Stephanie's husband, the Honorable George T. Weatherly, maintained an insanely expensive annual membership at the chi-chi Hillside Golf and Country Club, and had done so for decades. Steph joked that it would have been cheaper to buy it outright.

"We should own this damned golf course by now."

Giggling like schoolgirls, Missy, Teresa, and Stephanie, who represented three consecutive generations—hoisted their shot glasses. Pausing, the laughter sputtered out as the friends looked into each others eyes.

Despite the lighthearted ambiance, the ladies were there to celebrate a solemn occasion: Missy's unscathed survival. When she'd called Stephanie to tell her what had happened, she'd already heard. She'd found out through a frantic Teresa who, in turn, heard it on the local news.

The irony caused Missy to crack the teensiest of smiles. *Luke always said he'd be a headliner one day...*

Words were redundant. With a hearty chorus of *CHEERS!* and an All-For-One clank worthy of *The Three Musketeers,* the shooters were dispatched in a single, collective gulp.

The giggling began anew as Missy and Stephanie sucked lemons in an attempt to intercept the tequila fireballs heading straight for their bellies. Teresa, far and away the best 'shot' amongst them, declined the accoutrement. She sneered in the general direction of the traditional salt starters and lemon chasers, referring to them as 'training wheels for amateurs'. *Dah-links!*

While the amateurs guzzled back half of their sparkling water, Teresa summoned a waitress for a second round.

Begging off from another shooter, both Missy and Stephanie kicked it down a notch to fruity 'brelly' drinks. Teresa, the saucy, sophisticated, and often salty owner of Boutique Ebony & Ivory, ordered herself a Hendricks martini.

"Heavy on the Hendricks, love-y."

They all ordered food. While Teresa and Steph ordered dinner, Missy stuck to a stuffed mushroom appetizer, and that only to appease her pushy ex-boss.

Truth was, Missy wasn't hungry.

Although she could never share the goriest, or *glorious,* details with her friends, there was an excellent reason for her late arrival and lack of appetite...

Chapter 10

James had been in a playful mood, his stomach full, his cock well-tended. Missy knelt on the floor between his feet, content almost to the point of purring.

What was astonishing was how naturally she assumed the exacting position. With the grace of a ballerina, she'd settled onto her heels, chin held high, eyes cast down. Her hands rested atop her thighs in traditional submissive fashion, palms up and open in symbolic offering. She made sure to cinch her shoulders back, which in turn caused her fly-swatted breasts to push forward in the exaggerated fashion James favored.

Last but not least, she opened her legs and shut her mouth.

Steeped in an implausible sense of accomplishment, Missy basked in the warmth of his silent approval. The calm was all-pervasive, a cocoon of contentment amidst a world of chaos. *Sub-space.* She could float there forever, exhausted from a life spent pretending to be something she wasn't.

Naked, her swollen charms were on lewd display. The fluffy towel she'd wrapped herself in after the bath was a long-forgotten pile on the floor beside her. She would have sworn the knot gave way a split second before James touched it.

"No secrets and no privacy, little one..."

His long ago promise reverberated in her mind. Between her legs, her Master's cum co-mingled with her own and seeped from her body.

Submissive...

Installed in her mouth for the second time was the loathsome fly swatter. She'd assumed that James forgot his earlier directive to not drop it. Instead, he'd simply bided his time before addressing her infraction.

She was fast learning that in his world – *their world*— obedience was rewarded whereas disobedience was met with an endless array of dark and delicious disciplines. It was a simple enough concept. In theory. The pulse-pounding question was when each might be delivered. This one unknown component managed to keep her wet and wondering, perched on the proverbial edge of her seat.

Or heels, in her case.

Whore!

Her jaw was starting to ache. Also, there was nothing to be done about the disconcerting strings of saliva which escaped her lips to dribble down her chin and pool between her thighs.

Ever-so-faintly, her phone pinged from the other room. Barely audible even to her attuned ears, it was the third such ping in less than an hour. Missy frowned. She'd already spoken with her circle of friends and family, small as it was.

Oh, how she'd dreaded telling Christopher about his father's break in and resulting arrest. She did her best to sugar-coat it, but Christopher would have none of it. He'd insisted on speaking with James, who outlined the facts in black and white.

Christopher's voice boomed through the phone, its depth a testament to the fact that her little boy was growing up. A weight was lifted from her shoulders when he agreed that Luke was right where he belonged, adding a few choice words of his own to underscore.

Her heart swelled in her chest, filled to overflowing for the two incredible men in her life. She swallowed back the surge of emotion as her son thanked James again and again, his voice husky with gratitude. It was clear that he understood the dire ramifications had James arrived but a moment later.

At last, he'd asked to speak with his mom again. Before kiss-kiss-kissing him goodbye, Missy reminded him of her visit the following weekend. His first semester at college was about to begin and his seventeenth birthday coincided almost to the day. She intended to be there to celebrate both auspicious occasions. She missed her son every single day.

"Let me know what you need, baby. I'll either bring it up with me or we'll hit the mall when I get there."

As a farewell, she invoked the endearment they'd shared since he was a toddler.

"You know I love you *thiiis* much!"

Christopher had returned the endearment in kind and hung up.

No, these calls were not from Christopher. She'd know his ring, would swear to it on a stack of bibles. These calls had a menacing tone to them. They caused her Spidey-senses to tingle. Someone was intent on reaching her, and *not* content with giving her a chance to return their call.

Concerned, but not to the point of alarmed, Missy had put the calls out of her mind. Considering the man-scape before her, it hadn't been a difficult task...

35

Chapter 11

James sat in his favorite chair, going over some papers and squeezing a ball meant to work forearms. Every so often she caught a glimpse of one of his, and it was bulging.

The thought of those muscular arms around her was so exquisite, she moaned around the maddening contraption between her teeth.

He wore a plush terry robe with nothing underneath. While it was cinched at the waist, it gaped open from that point down, following the line of his splayed legs. His drained genitalia rested just over the chair's edge, in direct line with her lowered eyes. Missy was so close, she could see his depleted balls churning. Fascinated, she wondered at their ability to replenish, especially considering the magnitude and multitude of James' recent orgasms.

She chuckled at the bizarre direction of her thoughts. Of late, destiny's twists and turns were nothing less than staggering, delivering her to this precise moment in time. While the journey had been arduous, the destination fulfilled her utterly. Free of shame and guilt, she was infused with an almost unbearable lightness of being. She could think of worse ways to wile away the hours than on her knees speculating at the miracle of sperm reproduction.

In truth, she couldn't care less that his cock was flaccid and his balls empty. It wouldn't matter to her if he never achieved an erection again. Her feelings for this man transcended the physical act of sex. They emanated from places even his imposing phallus couldn't penetrate.

James was the long lost and longer missed piece of her soul, as she was his. Each was essential to the other, as symbiotic as sunshine and flowers. James knew exactly where her submissive buttons were located. They took equal and opposite pleasure in his pushing them.

Master...

He hadn't looked or spoken a word in her direction since they'd finished eating. Technically, James ate whereas she'd been fed. Missy sat with her hands clasped in her lap, mouth agape like a baby bird anticipating a fat, juicy worm. Morsels of fluffy omelet, bacon, and hash browns were fed to her by her Master's hand. She'd scarcely swallow one before his insistent fingers were pressing another to her lips.

James was intent on fattening her up, asserting she have three more bites even after she was full. He counted them down like a parent coercing a disinterested child, complete with zany faces and hilarious sound effects. While she giggled at his antics, she also felt a deep sadness that he'd never gotten to experience fatherhood.

The life-altering death of his young wife took care of that.

The third and final morsel was a juicy orange slice, which James placed between his teeth. She leaned forward to claim it and their lips met. Never had an ordinary orange slice tasted so divine. It was passed back and forth between their lips, masticated by both as their tongues embraced. Missy swallowed the shredded remnants as though manna from heaven.

Master...

For dessert, James wrapped her bruised tits around his cock and jerked himself off between them. The evidence of his satisfaction was now congealed on her chest. It made its cold, slimy way down her stomach in rivulets.

The longer James denied her his attention, the more intensely she hungered for it. Missy didn't dare speak for risk of loosing the fly swatter. Beginning to fidget, it took every bit of self-control she could muster to not simply lay her cheek against his knee.

It was then that the ball slipped from James' fingers and rolled away. At long last, he broke his silence. With a solitary syllable, he managed to produce an army of goosebumps...

"FETCH!"

Chapter 12

FETCH?

The range of deviant implications the usually benign word invoked boggled her mind. Missy's entire body ignited. If her nerve endings weren't zigging, they were zagging.

She was sure she was going straight to hell when her pulse began trip-hammering and her nipples stiffened to the approximate density of pencil erasers.

Whore!

Papers rustled as he set them aside, the sound as amplified in her ears as her heartbeat. Sight unseen, she knew the moment his attention shifted in her direction. The heat emanating from his gaze was palpable as it ferreted out her every nook and cranny. Missy micro-corrected her posture under his scrutiny, almost swooning when her efforts were rewarded.

"That's my good girl!"

Her exposed sex hammered between her thighs, swollen from use and slick with desire. Yet, when he proceeded to pat her on the head as one might a beloved labra-doodle, the near swoon came *this* close to a full-on faint. He must have sensed her confusion. James removed the fly swatter from her mouth just in time for her jaw to drop. His next words moved her to the brink of tears. It was as though he knew how much she needed to hear them.

"Little one, your Master is presumptuous enough to believe he knows your deepest and darkest desires. Your body language speaks volumes and every syllable is carefully assimilated. That being said, I am not so arrogant as to not take precautions."

She felt the need to reassure him.

"I trust you, sir. Beyond a shadow of a doubt. You must know."

He cupped her chin ever-so-gently, heedless of the gobs of saliva coating it. She felt his eyes boring into the crown of her skull, penetrating to read her most private thoughts as though highlighted for his convenience.

"I do know, pet. Even so, if I should happen to miscalculate, you are charged with the responsibility of speaking up and out. *Emphatically.* While I believe that safe-words are necessary amongst newbies and extremists, I have no use for them. I am not a sadist. I have no desire to push you beyond your tolerance or cause you undue pain."

His thumb traced the line of her jaw, dipping down to rest against her throat. Her carotid artery surged against it, speaking to the hot blood that raced through her veins at his lightest touch. James, whether loving and tender or demanding and Dominant, left her weak and wanting.

Submissive...

Enveloped in a bubble of belonging, Missy savored his final words on the subject.

"My only desire is to love you, protect you, and of course— fill the empty crevices in your sweet, submissive soul."

She was still trying to swallow the lump of emotion lodged in her throat when James leaned forward and unceremoniously shoved three fingers into her raw pussy. Grunting her shock, she came *this* close to dropping the fly swatter!

Evidently, with the loving reassurances out of the way, he saw no reason to dilly-dally. Over the lewd sloshing of her cum-drenched sex, James issued his first directive. His voice was as deep and smooth as midnight velvet, lulling her. The words he chose were another matter. Delivered ever-so-mundanely, he might well have asked for the salt to the passed.

But, he wasn't. Not even close...

"Eyes up, little one. Master enjoys watching you squirm while he's finger-fucking you."

Cheeks ablaze, Missy raised her gaze from his churning ballsac. It caught for a moment on the fullness of his lips before fixating on the fathomless depths of his eyes. Spellbound, she free-fell into them, his love her only safety net.

His next words snapped her back to full attention. While each was innocuous enough, together they caused the hair on the back of her neck to stand at attention.

"I'm in the mood to play a little game, pet. Doesn't that sound like fun?"

It was clear from the lilt in his voice that he was deriving great satisfaction from her discomfiture. Speaking of deriving satisfaction, she was no slouch in the department. The walls of her sopping hole grasped at James' trio of digits with such enthusiasm, one might surmise she was attempting to tear them from their sockets.

They sawed into her several more times before he withdrew them, only to hold them before her face. She was either unable or unwilling to tear her eyes from the glistening digits, all three covered in her own gooey discharge.

Without encouragement from James, she licked them clean. Pleased with her initiative and execution, he used the same fingers to point towards the strayed exercise ball.

"Now, go fetch girl!

Chapter 13

It was Teresa who steered the perfectly enjoyable conversation into something completely different. After a little gossip and a lot of laughter, the mood once again turned somber.

The pool-side eatery at Hillside Golf and Country Club was still bustling, despite the setting of the late-summer sun. The three women capped off their reunion with a selection of specialty coffees. Missy's and Stephanie's cafe au laits were lost under mountains of whipped cream. The bawdy Teresa sipped a cappuccino strong enough to grow hair on her chest. Instead of whipped cream, she topped it off with a shot of brandy.

And so it began.

"I've been meaning to tell you, dear. Lately, Ethan seems even more eccentric than usual, if that's possible. I'm getting a bad vibe when he comes into the boutique. He doesn't even pretend to shop anymore. Just wanders around, asking after you. One second he's a lovelorn Lothario, the next, he's fuming at what he calls 'the rejection'. Tell her, Stephanie."

While Missy was already determined to stay the hell away from Ethan, her friend's troublesome words served to underscore her decision. The man was koo koo for cocopuffs, at least where she was concerned.

Not missing a beat, Stephanie picked up where Teresa left off. Her eyebrows were knitted with concern.

"It's true, Missy. He's always struck me as a bit off, but, he's gone from peculiar to almost...menacing. That's the best way I can describe it. He was in every day last week. At least, he was on the days I worked."

Stephanie paused, looking from Missy to Teresa and back again. Missy knew the two women traveled in the same social circles and were much more than employer-employee.

"I've told Teresa she should ban him from E&I. He's strange at best, and seems to be quickly devolving. In any case, there's no doubt he's obsessed with you. I hope you steer clear of that one. You've had enough turmoil in your life."

Obsessed. The word twanged against an already raw nerve. Missy's skin crawled across her scalp. She'd been so wrapped up in her own misery, she missed the nuances. Instead, she'd invited him into her home where she proceeded to mount him like a rabid bitch in heat.

Missy sighed, mentally shaking her head. She was not fond of that particular memory but wasn't about to curl up in shame over it, either. He certainly hadn't complained at the time. In any case, shit happened. She could think of worse things that might have befallen the poor man.

Yet, since she'd fled from the restaurant mid-date, Ethan had erupted in near incoherent rage. *Slut, trailer trash,* and *skank* were just a few of the highlights that stood out from his rambling missives. His over-reaction would be laughable, if he weren't one of the most powerful, influential – *and obsessed*—men in town. Despite the 'God's-gift-to-women' image he worked overtime to sell, his actions spoke of a vengeful juvenile rebuffed by the one girl he vowed to have.

"Girls, he's sending me ugly texts. Really ugly."

As one, her friends faces changed from disturbed to appalled. Missy told them everything. Everything she knew, at least.

"Yeah. They started last night but I didn't notice until this afternoon. I was planning on calling him to explain, but that was *before* I listened to them. Now, I feel like he's the one who needs to apologize. Not that the overgrown baby would ever see it that way. Yes, it was rude to run out on him, but it was either that or throw up in his prime rib."

Missy speculated that if that were the case, his reaction would have been much the same. Based on the tone of his messages, he was a walking wick in search of a spark.

Steph and Teresa were nodding in unison, commiserating. They put their heads together to dissect the new details she'd divulged. Sipping at the dregs of their coffees, Teresa lit a rare cigarette. With that, a picture of Luke crawling on top of her flashed into her head, his breath heavy with alcohol and stinking of nicotine.

She shook it off, annoyed with herself. After all, this was the respected and successful Ethan Montgomery III they were talking about, not the down and out Luke Weaver. One could rot in jail and nobody would notice. The other had a reputation to maintain. Imagine was everything to Ethan. Much of his time, effort, and ego were invested in its maintenance. There was no way he'd risk it over a bad date.

So, when James had asked who was calling so often, she'd been honest. For the most part. He'd been upset enough about Luke as it was. She hadn't wanted to burden him with something that would turn out to be nothing. Ethan's outburst was just a bad case of spoiled rotten complicated by a flare-up of immaturity. He'd cool off when the tantrum passed.

"It's Ethan, sir. Ethan Montgomery. Do you remember him? I introduced you at The Pitts the other night. He's...wondering where I disappeared to so suddenly. And, why."

Connected at the soul, she'd sensed James' aura darken as he digested the information. His pupils constricted as dark storm clouds gathered on the horizon. Yet, other than a single vein pulsating at his temple, his features had remained inscrutable.

He'd nodded, but spoken not a word. Missy could only guess that he considered the entire episode behind and beneath them.

And, it was. She was positive...

Chapter 14

"There's something else that's been niggling at me, girls. Ethan seemed to know an awful lot about the assault. He said something along the lines of 'maybe he should have paid twenty-five thousand dollars for my...'services'."

Twenty-five thousand dollars. The exact amount payable on the check Luke slipped into his back pocket. The existence of that check was *not* public knowledge.

Stranger still, when she and James stopped at the house to pick up her car and a change of clothes, that same check was sitting on the kitchen counter. *Even if it fell out of Luke's pocket, it wouldn't have wound up on the counter.*

Missy was stupefied. How was it possible...?

Their waitress arrived with the check and a sweet smile, interrupting her train of thought. Stephanie, the only club member at the table, beamed back at her, signing off on the tab with a flourish. The tip must have been generous. The hard-working girl actually hugged her!

Smiling, Missy gathered her belongings and began the usual hunt for her car keys. Rummaging in the deepest corners of her purse, she bit her tongue to keep from screeching out in pain.

Under the table, Teresa was kicking her in the shin with her pointed, five-inch stiletto. And, three times in quick succession meant it was no accident. Jerking her leg away and her head up, Missy opened her mouth to voice her acute displeasure.

Following the direction of Teresa's flashing eyes, she stopped short, pain forgotten, friend forgiven...

Ethan Montgomery made a beeline for their table, a Goliath of a woman on his arm. They wore matching sneers of arrogant disdain, which they tried and failed to pass off as smiles. The results were macabre.

The woman was like none Missy had ever laid eyes on. In fact, she questioned whether the term 'woman' even applied. That she was able to out-vulgar Ethan was something in and of itself. His pompadour, Armani suit, and glittering jewels were contrived to capture center stage.

Yet, beside *that*, he faded almost to the status of nondescript.

As tall or taller than Ethan, she must have stood six-three, six-four. Her eyes were icy blue, and glacial cold. Where Medusa's crowning glory was a mass of venomous snakes, this creature was endowed with a mass of platinum dreadlocks that hung well below her corseted waist.

If possible, her heels were even higher than Teresa's. As gauche and out of place as they were, Missy could tell the calfskin thigh-highs were of the finest leather. Stretching well beyond her knees, they reached for, but failed to meet, the almost indictable hemline of her blood red bandage dress.

On the other extreme, her overblown cleavage threatened to jump ship with every juddering step she took. Missy was sure they'd make their escape before reaching their table. One bulging bicep was tattooed with some kind of whip, the tentacles of which reached over her shoulder to wind around her throat!

Missy shivered. Any beauty that might have been present in her statuesque carriage or long, well-muscled legs was lost in the threatening aura that radiated from her in waves.

Dominatrix! The word might as well have been stamped on the floozy's forehead. Missy was surprised how effortlessly it sprung to mind. She wasn't aware the word was part of her vocabulary.

The boisterous but conservative members of the Hillside Golf and Country Club were collectively struck dumb. Missy gasped, and not from pain. She wondered whether Teresa had kicked her to warn her of Ethan's suspicious arrival, or his companion's hideous ensemble.

Either way, the two of them together were a surreal sight indeed. Missy's ears rang as though a firetruck was in her head. The entire episode was surreal, over so quickly she wasn't sure she'd exhaled.

"Well, well, well. If it isn't the gracious proprietress of Ebony & Ivory. And her minions."

Ostensibly speaking to Teresa, his eyes bored into Missy's. Straightening her spine, she returned the stare. As shook up as she was, she didn't flinch and refused to blink. After her bully of an ex-husband, she wasn't about to let another man intimidate her.

"What the fuck are you doing here Ethan?"

It was Teresa, her blunt query doing nothing to disrupt the silent face off.

Ethan blinked first, turning to Teresa with an exaggerated bow. Smarmy smirk in place, he sidestepped her pointed question. Instead, he commented on her *'glorious'* head scarf. Not one to be side-tracked, Teresa gave his companion the once over. Twice.

"Aren't you going to introduce us to this...?"

Her sarcastic tone and judgmental eyes screamed *TRAMP!* There was no need to finish the sentence. Once again, Ethan declined to take the bait. The 'tramp' in question stood unperturbed, a silent, malevolent presence.

"Always a pleasure to see you ladies. Please forgive the intrusion."

Tipping an imaginary hat, Ethan took his companion's arm. Turning to leave, his last words were almost, but not quite, inaudible.

"I'm sure we'll meet again soon..."

Chapter 15

Pity you decided to do away with your collar, pet. I could have attached a leash to it and taken you for a nice walk.

James sat on the back deck of his old Victorian manse, cigar in one hand, cognac in the other. A light breeze rustled the leaves of the forest-like foliage that surrounded him on three sides. An oft sought haven of beauty and tranquility, he was finding it difficult to appreciate either.

Evidently, his nervous system was yet to receive the memo that Missy was out of danger. For some reason he could not put a finger on, he remained on edge, reflexes coiled and primed for action.

The fact that she was out and about so soon after her harrowing ordeal did nothing to alleviate his sense of unease. He far preferred his precious whore where she belonged - at his feet, where he could best watch over her.

Alas, that was not the case. Recalling her reaction to his scandalous words was an excellent second choice, tantalizing enough to bring a lecherous grin to his lips. Once she'd digested their meaning, her head whipped around at lightning speed, eyes the size of platters. The outright shock on her distorted face caused his tired cock to stir.

She'd known better than to speak, not that she'd been able to with the exercise ball lodged in her mouth. In this game, words were off-limits. For Missy, at least. A nice, enthusiastic *WOOF!* was her only available means of communication. While he was disappointed that she hadn't availed herself of the option, it only meant he had something to look forward to.

After all, today he'd introduced it as an option. That wouldn't always be the case.

Missy was fetching, in every sense of the word. He was taken with the fluid grace of her gait as it juxtaposed with the froth of saliva that clung to her chin. She retrieved the squeeze-ball time and time again. In fact, she retrieved it until her sides heaved. Until her entire body glistened. Until she panted with the proof of her efforts.

Missy fetched until his cock couldn't help but take notice. It rose up from the dead like a phoenix from the ashes.

She fetched until she got it right and she did so with fervor. The creamy moisture between her legs never once dissipated. Just the opposite, in fact. She literally gushed, much like the hydrants that four-legged retrievers found so appealing.

If she'd a tail, it would have been wagging!

That titillating notion had been the turning point. His cock had distended to its very limits, vibrating like a tuning fork. In his mind, James revisited the exquisite feeling of his cum-heavy balls tightening as blood surged through gnarled, overtaxed veins. The tip turned an angry shade of purple in under three seconds. Another thirty, and the entire head had been slathered in a protective layer of slimy pre-cum. To say that he'd been prepared was an understatement. Like a naughty Boy Scout, James had been *'up'* for anything!

Grinning still, James took a puff of cigar and washed it down with a healthy swig of cognac. Feeling much more at ease, he relaxed into the chaise lounger and blew several perfect smoke rings into the dusk. As they wafted into nothingness, he thanked the powers-that-be that Missy's submissive nooks fit his Dominant crannies to a T.

The proud sparkle in her eye when she'd deposited the ball at his feet was the proof. Her swollen, sodden cunt was the pudding!

Submissive...

Chapter 16

A good Dominant knows when his submissive has had enough.

James puffed his dying cigar back to life and scratched his balls. He knew when *his* submissive has had enough, of that he was confident. He perceived Missy's needs as though the road map was stamped into his DNA.

Polite society would never understand, but theirs was truly the perfect fusion, right up there with bricks and mortar, thunder and lightning—chocolate and peanut butter. Intrinsically, he'd known that the simple act of depriving her of his attention would keep her wet, wanting, and whimpering.

What *she* didn't know was that it was just as arduous for him as it was for her. He enjoyed engaging with her on every level and on any topic. Missy was the total package: smart, sexy, and of course, submissive. That being said, there was no doubt that their private world of TPA (*Total Power Exchange) was the highlight. The glue.

The icing on the cake of their lives.

Amused at the cliche, James sucked a cognac infused ice cube and tried another: If he were a bowl of cherries, Missy was his whipped cream topping.

Or, in their case – bottom!

She was certainly put through her paces this day. Not only did she learn to fetch, but also to sit, lie down, and even to roll over. When she executed the trick to his satisfaction, James would scratch behind her ear or rub her belly. Missy's eyes lit up each time, often accompanied by a heartwarming whimper.

Wholly engaged, there was no doubt she'd fancied their naughty diversion. At one point, her tongue had lolled out as she panted in anticipation of his throwing the ball.

"Good girl!"

The pride that shone from her magnificent eyes had been blinding. He'd requested that she resume her kneeling position at his feet. Removing the ball from her slobbering mouth, he'd replaced it with the dreaded fly swatter once again. Her expression changed dramatically. It was clear she'd believed herself free of the annoying, teat-smacking instrument.

James had responded to the question written all over her face.

"To the crux of the matter, my dear. Consider this a lesson and a reward all wrapped into one. This time, however, I suggest you *not* drop it!"

Her breath came in ragged gasps, his big toe buried to the hairy hilt in her sloppy wet slit. The very sight of her moved him. Her hair hung in curls around her make-up-free face while her saucer-wide eyes offered easy access to the essence of her being. Cliche or no cliche, this woman completed him.

Stroking his dick in front of her face, he measured his progress. Timing was everything. After all, it was so much more romantic when two lovers came as one. He'd made the most of necessary interludes by painting her face fifty shades of pre-cum.

Twice, he was forced to remove his burrowing digit in order to lubricate a dry, shaft-chafing palm. Both times, he managed to replace it without missing a stroke. The boney knuckle clipped her clit with each thrust as the calloused toe-pad probed for her g-spot.

"Masturbate for me baby. Show me how you touch yourself when you're alone in the dark."

A sharp intake of breath was one sign that she'd heard him. Her hand making its tentative way to her pussy was another. The turmoil in her eyes spoke to a sudden and acute discomfiture. James found it interesting that she would eagerly crawl on all four's to fetch a ball, but drew the line at touching herself for his viewing pleasure.

The hard-wired remnants of a religious upbringing, perhaps?

He'd stopped jerking off then, and taken her heart-shaped face into his hands. Whispering hot breath into her ear, he'd told her what she already knew, but needed to hear again.

"There is no pious judgment here, my sweet. At my feet, you are free of society's shackles and emancipated within mine. Your coyness is unfounded. You are home, you are safe, and you are mine."

Verbally incapacitated, Missy nodded her understanding, curls bouncing, eyes shining. Satisfied that her angst was put to rest, he kissed the tip of her nose and leaned back. Taking a firm grip of his still firm member, he leered crudely.

"Now, let's get on with it, shall we, pet? I'm about ready to blow!"

Chapter 17

And the rest, as they say, was history.

Missy kneaded that fattened nubbin with primitive abandon, fingers more adept than any vibrator. Half of his size eleven foot had been coated in the viscous liquid that spewed non-stop from her hole. When the walls of her cunt began to spasm around his wriggling toe, he'd known the time had come – and Missy was about to.

Her hissing breath escalated into a single keening moan that seemed to go on forever. Her lips curled back, exposing bared teeth clamped vice-like around the shaft of the swatter. There was no way she was dropping it this time.

The sight of her grinding and grunting in the throes of an animalistic orgasm was more than any god could expect any mere mortal to withstand.

James was undone.

His roar of release was deafening. A torrent of spunk erupted from his lurching cock to splatter her features. It seemed to go on forever. Yet, undeterred by the thick jism dripping down her face, Missy's hips continued to buck against his toe.

Her gnashing pussy had swallowed it whole and still wanted for more!

From his place on the back deck, James heard Missy's car circle the front driveway. He tucked the delightful memories away for safekeeping, readily available to replay at his leisure. Right now, however, he was just thankful that Missy was back without incident.

He frowned, acknowledging his acute apprehension was unbecoming of a Master. Still, it was not borne of insecurity, but of tragedy. After all, his sweet Angeline had died in his arms. And, just yesterday, he could have lost Missy.

All things considered, it wasn't a big surprise that angst still lingered.

Angst wasn't about to get in the way of his game plan, mind you. He meant to have the woman he loved wearing his collar once again and the sooner the better. *This* time, he'd make damned sure she understood the full spectrum of implications and obligations.

While he'd hit the high notes the first time, he admitted to erring in that arena. He could have, and should have, delved deeper. He'd taken his cues from Missy's level of submissiveness, which was off the charts. He should have been more attuned to her level of experience. Which was nil.

A natural submissive was much like unformed clay. While flush with untapped potential, if not scrupulously forged she could easily become damaged in the unforgiving kiln that was the world of Dominance and submission.

With that edict in mind, James didn't budge from his comfortable chaise lounger. Didn't move a muscle when the engine of her car cut nor after the door slammed. Enjoying the last of his cigar, James waited for several sharp raps of the brass knocker before finally rousing himself and heading for the door.

No, it would benefit neither to allow this one-of-a-kind woman to deter him from his Master plan. Not that there was much risk of that happening. The truth was that as his feelings for her deepened, his desire to dominate her heightened.

Perfect...

Of course, one day he intended to give Missy her own key.

The day she earned her collar back.

His grin reappeared just as he slid back the bolt...

Chapter 18

Laying beside her, James pulled her bottom tight against him, spoon style. One arm encircled her waist, holding her close. The other supported her head, his hand reaching around to gently cup her breast. He buried his face in the hollow between her shoulder and neck. Her pulse thrummed against his lips.

Kissing his way up to her ear, he tongued it inside and out before whispering into it.

"Sweet dreams, little one."

The entire length of her body was in contact with his, her feet tangled between and around his muscular calves. She wriggled her naked backside into him for warmth, inadvertently igniting another kind of fire.

The heat began between her butt cheeks where his cock was nestled, but soon permeated every fiber of her being. *Oh god, would she ever stop yearning for this man's touch?*

Applying pressure to her breast, James chuckled against her ear, warning her of the 'consequences' for rousing his bone-weary cock. She chuckled back, adding one last exaggerated wriggle before settling in.

Now, his heart tatted against her back in a slow, rhythmic sleeping pattern.

Hers, on the other hand, was racing. As was her mind. Sleep was beaten back whenever it ventured near, adrenaline winning every skirmish.

When she'd arrived, James took her hand and led her into the darkened kitchen. Together they'd fixed a pot of hot tea. In one motion, he'd lifted her onto the counter, peeled off the panties she'd worn to meet the girls, and opened her legs.

Bare-chested and beautiful, he'd taken his place between them. He'd showered in her absence. The scent of aftershave was so elusive it served only to madden her senses. His innate confidence, cat-like grace, and bulging biceps were a one, two—three punch that stole her breath away.

He'd stolen her heart the moment they met.

Master...

Their voices hushed and heads together, conversation had flowed as easily as the tea. Silences were golden, never awkward. It felt as natural as breathing, reinforcing her belief that their union was predestined, perhaps even lifetimes in the making.

Missy was home. In every sense of the word.

James had brushed a stray strand of hair from her eyes. When he'd tucked it behind her ear, she leaned her head against his palm.

"I'm sorry, little one, but I can't join you and Christopher next weekend. You know how much I was looking forward to us spending time as a family, but I find myself up to my armpits in paperwork with deadlines fast approaching. I promise to make it up to you both."

Family. Her ears had picked up on the word like a bat honed in on sustenance. It's what she always wanted, an old fashioned family unit. While she'd been disappointed on the one hand, on the other she was thrilled. She'd seen the work piling up on his desk. She also knew the reason he'd been distracted.

Grinning, she'd teased him, "Neglecting your work, sir? I can't imagine why."

She'd turned her head to kiss his palm, speaking against it.

"I'm terribly disappointed, of course, sir. But, Christopher and I will be fine on our own. We've had plenty of practice in that department."

Placing his mug aside, he'd taken her face in both hands and kissed her. With his lips still pressed to hers, he'd reached into his jeans pocket and pulled out the fine silver choker he'd given her once-upon-a-time. Holding it in two fingers before her eyes, it sparkled in the dim light, heart pendant gently twirling. She'd cried happy tears when he fastened it around her neck.

Now, laying the length of this magnificent man, she fingered the chain, deep in thought.

She'd regaled James with stories of her visit with the girls. She hadn't, however, mentioned Ethan. She needed time to process his sudden appearance.

Was it just a coincidence?

She took comfort in the fact that he was with a woman...of sorts. *That has to be a good sign, doesn't it?* Plus, there were no more messages. A very good sign, indeed.

Safe in the arms of the man she adored, Missy decided to let it go. If Ethan started up again, she wouldn't hesitate to let James deal with him. With that settled, Missy's eyelids began to droop.

One last wriggle and she was fast on her way to meeting James in Dreamland...

Chapter 19

That twat has humiliated me for the last time!

Ethan slouched in the sumptuous pedicure chair, more hung over than usual. Massaging rollers kneaded his entire backside, alternating between soothing caresses and stimulating karate-type 'chops'. A young Asian girl sat on a stool at his feet, shaving the dead skin from his soles. A second applied hot wax to his hands in preparation for a clear coat of polish.

He ogled the illiterate bitches from head to toe, deeming them both do-able. In fact, they elicited fond memories of his most recent visit to Thailand. Miserable as he was, he managed to chuckle.

Ethan enjoyed mixing business with pleasure, especially in foreign locales where he could indulge his more violent whimsies. Often, he was on a private jet heading home before the slut – *or sluts* – even regained consciousness.

The young, fuck-able aesthetician on the stool tapped his ankle, a signal to switch feet. Ethan did so mechanically, engrossed in sweet recollection. Those two Thai hookers weren't so pretty by the time he was done with them. In fact, the homelier one would probably never turn another trick.

While he preferred to play on more 'forgiving' soil, Missy Weaver's blatant lack of respect would provoke any man in any country. She might as well have waved a red cape in front of an angry bull. He'd sat in that fucking restaurant for half a fucking hour before it even dawned on him that she wasn't fucking coming back.

It took another thirty minutes for his blood pressure to drop back into the safe zone. He was surprised his eyeballs hadn't pop right out of his head.

He wound up at a crappy strip club in a crappier neighborhood. The best dressed mark for miles, he hadn't wanted for attention. More than a tad lubricated, he was blocks from home when he pulled a sudden U-y.

Fuck her! The ill-mannered cow had earned herself a good slap and he meant to deliver it personally.

Those plans changed when he turned onto her street.

Well into the wee hours of the morning, a gaggle of curious neighbors were congregated on the sidewalk in front of Missy's house, housecoats wrapped tightly about them. A cop car was just pulling out of the driveway, lights flashing. A man was in the back seat, his dazed, doughy face pressed against the reinforced glass.

The front door of the house looked like it'd been kicked in. Ethan wondered if someone had gotten to the bitch before him. *Surely, I'm not the only man she's fucked over.*

Curious, he'd slumped down in his seat, a feeble attempt to go incognito. His pimped out Maserati convertible stuck out like a sore thumb in the trailer-trash neighborhood. He'd noticed a fancy little Audi parked a ways up the hill. Also out of place on the dilapidated tract, he took an educated guess as to its ownership. It would appear that Mr. James Colton, the man she'd gone ga-ga over in the restaurant, was also in the house.

But, why was he parked so far away?

Curiouser and curiouser, Ethan had found an inconspicuous spot on the street and turned off the high-performance engine. Moments later, a carpenter's truck arrived and pulled into the driveway next to Missy's old Nissan.

Other than putting the top up, there was little Ethan could do to avoid detection. He put his faith in the cover of darkness to protect him. He knew that if he kept his eye on the prize, everything else would fall into place.

Hadn't it always?

Ethan Montgomery was not one to worry about shit he couldn't control.

Isn't that what the dumb-ass twelve-step program recommended?

Mulling over the precise wording of the AA mantra, he'd reached into one of the many hidden compartments that the luxury vehicle furnished. From it, he withdrew a bottle of four-hundred-dollar scotch whiskey. Careful to not spill on his Armani suit, he'd unscrewed the lid and swigged it straight.

The burst of soft honey and nutty caramel sat unappreciated on his palate. Unappeased, he guzzled again.

At last, he'd smiled. 'Unappeased' could be his middle name, it suited him so well. He had a penchant for all things expensive, no matter how gauche or gaudy. What he desired most were the few things in the world that were beyond his reach.

He felt he deserved them.

What he didn't feel was the need to delve into *why*, coming from money and wanting for nothing, he still wanted more. He wasn't much for self-examination. He left that to those tree-hugging, free-Willy, liberal-type bastards.

Without remorse, he catered to the twin monsters that inhabited his soul: Insecurity and Greed. He nourished the ravenous duo with two of their favorite dishes: Bigger and Better.

In many an alcoholic rage, Mother had warned him that these two unquenchable traits did not mesh well with his over inflated ego and sense of entitlement.

Well, thank you Mommy dearest, so glad you're dead.

Turning to his favorite jazz station, he'd taken yet another nip at the bottle. Settling back, he'd waited for the coast to clear...

Chapter 20

Despite the wicked hangover, Ethan's mind was always working. He wrapped his arms around the little Asian girls as they helped him hobble from the pedicure platform to the drying station. He knew the drill, but enjoyed the show as they twittered instructions using broken English and flailing arms. Placing his hands and feet under the blue lights to dry, he lost himself in his three favorite topics: himself, Missy Weaver, and revenge.

While his tootsies dried, Ethan drifted back to the night she'd sealed her own fate.

With the patience of Job and the assistance of Scotch, he'd surveilled the cunt's boarded up house. Eventually, the lights went out and two figures emerged as one. Missy leaned heavily against the Colton fellow's side, clutching the muscular arm that supported her. She was gazing up at him, unabashed adoration written all over her face.

Fucking slut.

Beads of perspiration erupted on Ethan's brow as hot flashes of hatred and jealousy engulfed him. He swore he'd know everything there was to know about the son of a bitch, and in very short order. Ethan had a lot of connections, on both sides of the law. Not to mention that he could no doubt buy and sell the man ten times over.

He watched as, after a quick conference with the carpenter, they climbed into the Audi and zoomed off into the night.

By the time the powerful motor was out of earshot, the carpenter was backing his truck out of the driveway and the gawkers were heading back to their beds.

At last...

With one final slug of liquid courage, Ethan exited the car, careful not to slam the door. It didn't take much to loosen the temporary boards and enter the ramshackled abode. Even so, he disliked the dirty work, hated getting his manicured hands dirty. He'd berated himself for not calling the boys.

The boys were an exclusive band of talented hooligans ranging from white collar to no collar. On each, he held a dossier of damning information. If push came to shove, he'd have no qualms using the material to crush them. He made sure they knew it as well, issuing 'friendly' reminders on a regular basis.

The looming threat of exposure tended to keep them loyal.

The tamper-proof location of the incriminating evidence tended to keep Ethan alive.

He realized the less enlightened might consider such tactics blackmail. From his point of view, they just made good business sense, profitable for all concerned. He simply offered 'incentives' that they couldn't – *for the life of them—* refuse.

In any case, it'd been too late for reinforcements. Opportunity had knocked and he'd answered. Re-focused on the task at hand, he'd clicked on the LED flashlight attached to his key chain and headed straight for the slut's bedroom...

Chapter 21

Missy trembled, legs weak. The hand holding the railing was white-knuckled.

Annoyed, she took a deep breath, forcing herself to release the death grip. She refused to be intimidated, even if she was scared shitless. Mounting the stairs of her new, pressure-treated front porch, she slid the key into her new, steel-enforced front door.

For the first time since her parents died, Missy had a support system on which to lean. A safety net in which to fall. On her knees at her Master's feet, she was empowered as never before. She suckled from his strength, to discover her own. She basked in his protection, to find courage in her heart.

Master...

This was her second homecoming since that horrendous night. On the first, James was by her side. Now, standing alone in the foyer, the trauma of Luke's attack hung heavy in the air. But, there was something else, as well. She'd noticed it the first time, but had been too overwhelmed to analyze it.

Aside from the stench of stale garbage and abject fear, Missy smelled Ethan Montgomery.

Courageous or not, the hairs on the back of her neck stood up. Cinching her shoulders back, she moved forward, a symbolic reclaiming of her own home. After all, it made sense that Ethan's scent would linger. She *did* spend the afternoon before the attack riding him like a bronco bull at a rodeo. And, he *did* wear enough cologne to pollute a small nation.

Missy made her way to Christopher's room. She'd stuck her nose in here many a time since he'd left, never failing to tear up. This was her baby's 'Cave'. It sat near-empty in the only home he'd ever known. And now, he was off to college and she...

She couldn't stay here!

Missy gathered what she came for and turned to leave. As she did, Christopher's old computer caught her eye. She recoiled, flashing back to a drunken day she'd rather forget. The blanket of foreboding that enveloped her as she typed the letters BDSM into the search bar was knitted into her memory banks. As was the feeling of utter hopelessness after she'd learned the truth: *Removing one's collar was a transgression of unpardonable proportion.* It was the BDSM equivalent of severing the relationship and considered irrevocable.

She'd known the full magnitude of James' feelings when he broke the time-honored credo and forgave her the unforgivable. He also assumed full responsibility for his own trespasses, promising to never repeat them. That being said, his eyes danced when he spoke of the debaucherous protocol he had in mind for her to earn back her collar.

She was thankful he'd refrained from mentioning the explosive gratification that *she* was sure to experience – *in multiples*—along the way. Even so, that indisputable truth hung in the air. James and she were two sides of the same coin. His 'Heads' balanced her 'tails' to the penny.

She might have smiled at the analogy, had a vision of herself masturbating at James' feet not leapt to mind.

Missy shook her head. *Of all things, that had thrown her?* She'd needed his reminder that society's shackles held no sway in their private world. With that reassurance, all bets were off. He'd kissed the tip of her nose and she'd gushed all over his foot.

Missy blushed. It was near impossible to believe that she, a once introverted and self-conscious woman, had proceeded to use that foot in conjunction with her hand to hump her way to a ferocious orgasm.

Whore!

Proud whore. What mainstream society saw as a blasphemous obscenity was, to her, a term of endearment. James took words that would trigger seizures in the unenlightened and transformed them into something beautiful. Sensual.

Romantic.

With her arms loaded, she hip checked Christopher's bedroom door closed behind her. One thing was indisputable. After James, there was no turning back. She'd found that out the hard way...

Chapter 22

What the hell is that?

After depositing her son's things on the kitchen counter, she headed to her room for a few of her own. James didn't own a blow dryer, never mind hair spray. He simply pumped some gel into his hands, and used his fingers to push his hair straight back.

Quite frankly, Missy thought it was one of the sexiest, most masculine gestures she'd ever witnessed. Sexier still was when his tresses refused to cooperate and fell back into his eyes.

She found herself staring off into nowhere with a stupid grin on her face. Missy gave herself an imaginary pinch. *Get with it, girl.* The weekend was fast approaching and there was much to accomplish. Dusting off her mental 'to-do' list, she scrolled.

The posters, books, and couple pairs of jeans Christopher asked for were now officially crossed off.

Tick...

She wanted to get him an extra set of sheets and a comforter. Not to mention a decent pillow. All on the list for today.

Tick...

She needed a birthday card, and she wanted it to be perfect. She was so proud of her brilliant boy, seventeen years old and already starting college. She couldn't lie, she still wished he'd found a school closer to home. In any case...

Tick...

She'd decided to buy his favorite birthday cake and take it with her. If it didn't get ruined on the close to four hour drive, it would be worth it to see the look on his face. It was already on order.

Tick, tick, tick...

Time was running out and here she was, daydreaming about James. Shaking her head in wonder, Missy put her sorry butt into gear. She'd decided it was for the best that he wasn't able to join them. She would miss him, of course, and Christopher was also disappointed. At the same time, she looked forward to a mother/son reunion. It seemed like forever since she'd seen him last.

Grabbing what she needed for the immediate future, she hustled for the door. She was just about through it when...

What the hell is that?

A jewel-blue scrap of material hung half in and half out of her wicker trash container. Bending down to take a closer look, her blood ran cold. She didn't need to see the monogrammed E.M.III to know the handkerchief belonged to Ethan. She'd seen it before. It'd been wrapped around his effeminate knuckles when he'd knocked on her shabby door.

But, how did it wind up in her bedroom?

He'd asked to use the bathroom after their...encounter. She remembered laughing out loud when he'd asked for 'directions'. Pointing down the only hallway in the miniscule house, she'd joked with him not to get lost.

Had he ducked into her bedroom instead? She wouldn't put it past the entitled son of a bitch. She envisioned a never ending supply of hand-woven hankies, in every hue imaginable. He probably tossed them away like tissue.

She could easily have missed it the first time. The day following Luke's break-in, just getting through the front door had taken every ounce of strength she could muster. Leaning on James for support, she might as well have been wearing blinders.

That was it! Missy stood, her pulse nearing normal. There was no other plausible explanation. She'd like to give the nosy prick a piece of her mind, but decided it prudent to let sleeping pricks lay. She hadn't seen or heard from Ethan since the initial barrage of nasty text messages.

No doubt, he'd forgotten about her long ago...

Chapter 23

They bowed and shuffled, two grateful cunts.

Ethan paid the slant-eyed sluts, magnanimously adding a dollar tip for each. As one got on her knees to slide sandals onto his feet, the other held open the door. His driver, Bobby, pulled up unlawfully close to the building. Ethan's feet never touched concrete.

Perfect...

He climbed into the back of the Hummer, a sure sign to leave him the fuck alone. His hangover felt better, and there were plans to make. He hadn't forgotten about Missy for a nano-second. Nor would he. Not until the thankless bitch was taught a lesson in respect.

If revenge was best served cold, Ethan wanted his frozen solid. Reaching into his pocket, he drew out a pair of Missy's panties. Holding the crotch area to his nose, he leaned back and smirked, inhaling her faint scent.

He'd located her bedroom without incident. Banging his shin in the tiny cubicle, his anger escalated. *How could he have lowered himself to such a level?*

He rifled through her meager wardrobe and under her ancient single bed. Finding nothing of interest, he'd moved on to her underwear drawer.

There was precious little that qualified as sexy – no corsets, no g-strings, no stockings. Nonetheless, there was a tangle of silken panties and several brassieres. There were even a few matched sets. He helped himself to a couple of the choicer items, not wanting to leave a noticeable void. He caught a quick sniff before pocketing them.

They would go nicely with the rest of his collection.

It wasn't until he was leaving that he spied the shopping bag from Ebony & Ivory Boutique. Since he spent more than his fair share of time in that fine establishment, he recognized the insignia immediately. In Missy's tattered room, it stuck out like a hunk of gold in a pile of shit.

He also recognized fine lingerie when he saw it. After all, he'd bought enough. Drawing out the stunning La Perla corset, he was appalled to find it ruined. Looking closer, he realized it was covered in semen stains. Ethan was sickened. He knew who's jism it was.

And who's it wasn't.

Dropping the disgusting garment, he'd scrubbed every finger with his monogrammed French-silk handkerchief. Holding it between two finger, he'd deposited it into the trash, contaminated beyond salvation.

Grimacing with distaste, he'd left the room as he found it and took three whole steps to the next.

A sign taped to the door read 'The Cave'—an apt description, as it turned out. Although it looked—and smelled, recently vacated, the posters of fast cars and near-naked women left no doubt that *this* cave had once been inhabited by a boy.

He vaguely recalled her mentioning a son that was headed off to college. The ill-mannered cow interrupted him to inject the useless information. Now, Ethan wracked his brain for the kid's name and the location of the college. There must be some way to use the intriguing nugget to his advantage.

He'd spied an ancient computer gathering dust in the corner and turned it on. It took longer for the fucking dinosaur to power up than it did for him to find out everything he needed to know.

From there, he'd moved into the minuscule space she called a living room. His eyes fell immediately to the threadbare couch. Memories flooded his cortex and Ethan's already considerable anger had gone through the shoddy roof!

His horny ass had been planted on that piece of shit couch, suit pants down around his ankles. He'd been ridden like the odds-on favorite at the Kentucky Derby, urged over the finish line in record-breaking time.

The memories outraged him. He hadn't suspected at the time that her sole purpose was to rid herself of his cock as expeditiously as possible. He'd been oblivious to the fact that he was nothing more than a pawn in her game to achieve her true goal – James Colton.

In the back of his chauffeur driven Hummer, Ethan crushed the panties in his hand, imagining Missy's windpipe. Stuffing the wisp of material back into his pocket, he glanced at his watch and took the expected call. Swiping the phone, he listened to the report and hung up without speaking a word. The slut had left her house and was pulling into a nearby shopping mall.

Updated hourly, Ethan's henchmen were working in shifts.

The way he saw it, the conman had been conned. As Bobby maneuvered the SUV down the ramp to the underground parking, Ethan was sure of two things: He was *not* going to be played the fool and he was *not* going to get over it.

Instead, Ethan was going to get even...

Chapter 24

Get home and get naked...

Missy did a double take, her brain needing a moment to correlate what her eyes were seeing. The phone pinged just as she was rushing to the car, her arms laden with packages. Now, sitting half in and half out of the vehicle, her fingers flew in response to James' text.

Yes, sir, my pleasure. Giggle. But...who's home?

She'd just left the shopping center where they first met, hallowed ground as far as she was concerned. She managed to cross nearly everything off the list, even finding the perfect no-occasion card for James.

On the front was a single rose—red, of course, thorns prominent. Tangled in it was a silver chain with a heart pendent, much like the one she wore around her own neck. The inside of the card was blank. She was going to try her hand at writing a poem.

The plan was to wait until the last second before giving it to him. She was pretty sure she couldn't write poetry worth a shit.

PING!

Missy forced herself to pull her legs into the car, shut the door, and slip the key into the ignition before tearing into the text.

No questions, whore. You'll find the door open.

And with that, Missy headed off in the appropriate direction, almost giddy. She hadn't seen James in hours, five at least. She needed a fix.

She wouldn't have noticed the Hummer except that it was on her short list of sexiest cars. If it were possible for a Hummer to pass for nondescript, this one came close. Monochromatic beige, there were no exterior markings. Even so, she was sure she'd seen it before. In this hood, Hummers were a rare sighting, whether a single shade of beige or fifty.

Her phone continued to ping on the twenty minute drive. Letting herself into James' house, she placed the packages on the velvet-upholstered bench at the entrance and grabbed for her cell. Devouring his words, her body flushed from head to toe. She'd swear her core temperature rose with each syllable.

First: *Follow the directions to the letter.*

Next: *Do not fail.*

And finally: *Master misses his whore.*

In response, her nipples tingled. Her Master-attuned pussy began to thrum. It started as a tiny ripple deep in her belly, but quickly grew into dizzying waves of desire. If she were a meteorologist, she'd brace for the approaching tsunami.

PING!

Take a piss and clean yourself in the guest bath. You'll find your butt-plug and some lube next to the sink. Use them. Make sure you take advantage of each and every inch.

Missy was dumbstruck. He wanted her to what? She couldn't possibly...

Her anus constricted and her mind spun at the thought of impaling herself. Vividly, she recalled her first encounter with the daunting apparatus. Laying face down across James' lap, he'd pulled it from his jacket pocket. Making sure she got a good look at it, he'd proceeded to demonstrate its usage.

Missy's face burned as though someone was holding a flamethrower to it. In her mind's eye, she watched herself reach around to open her ass cheeks to afford him easier access.

He'd left her house one butt plug lighter, having worked it into her virgin ass where it remained until she'd seen him next. At that memorable juncture, his rock hard cock had taken its place. Draped over the back of a sofa, unendurable pain was somehow transformed into the most exquisite pleasure.

She'd been left exhausted, slick with sweat. In and of itself, the experience had been staggering. Yet, staggering didn't begin to describe the anal orgasm that had ripped through her body and shredded her mind. Until that moment, she hadn't realized such things were even possible.

Whore!

Missy sat down on the bench next to her purchases, wobbly-kneed.

PING!

It should be in by now. Yes or no.

Missy scrambled back to the here and now. She all but flew down the hall to the bathroom where she squatted, peed, and washed herself. The easy part done, she texted a one word response.

Almost.

PING!

You have ninety seconds, whore. I'll be home...anytime...

Chapter 25

Dropping his briefcase on his desk, James immersed himself in the peace and tranquility of his home and castle.

It'd been one bitch of a day, spent in negotiations with the bloated, top-heavy CEO of Shindigo—a bloated, top-heavy corporation. Both were in desperate need of trimming. James outlined a strategy which included a pronounced decrease in upper management together with an A to Z retraining of the sales force. The result would pare the paunch as well as beef up the company's bottom line.

Now, it was a waiting game. Time would tell if the big man in the glass office had the stones to cut the pork.

Enough of that crap...

Dispensing with work, he slipped off his jacket, loosened his tie, and focused on more tantalizing topics. James envisioned the scene awaiting him just down the hall. The image of Missy lubing up her puckered butt hole brought a smile to his lips and a rush of hot blood to his groin.

He could just see her cunt dripping as she labored to cram the five-inch stainless steel plug up her tight little ass. Although it didn't play into this evenings plans, he looked forward to the day she would perform the wanton spectacle for his viewing pleasure.

James grinned as his cock lurched at the idea. Making a mental note, he readjusted his pants. All of a sudden, they were chafing.

It wasn't difficult to imagine her chaotic thoughts, knowing what was to come. The note he'd left in the bathroom left no room for doubt. He'd placed it under the lubricant, impossible to miss.

"You've been such a good girl, Master has decided to reward you with a nice ass fucking. We both remember how much you enjoyed your first reaming, don't we, my precious? Not to mention the orgasmic heights you attained."

"Once the plug is inserted, assume the proper position on Master's bed. The pillows are there to help lift your bottom to a more fuckable height. There's no need to thank me. Yet.

Masturbate. Do not come. Wait..."

While he'd slammed the door hard enough to wake the dead, James was in no hurry to join Missy in the bedroom. He'd simply wanted to announce his arrival. Anticipation was an hors d'oeuvre to be savored, never rushed. Looking at his watch, he estimated that Missy had been 'savoring' for close to forty minutes now.

Submissive...

He pictured her counting the seconds as she diddled her clit to the brink of orgasm again and again. By now, she'd be well marinated in her own juices. *Perfect!*

Another five minutes wouldn't hurt...

He made his way through the sprawling, one-story house, making sure every window and door was secure. Punching the code into the security system, he made a mental note to stop at the dry cleaners in the morning. Precum had managed to soak through two layers of material. The silver dollar sized stain on his light cotton slacks was expanding fast.

Apparently, Missy wasn't the only one marinating.

At last, he slipped into his darkened bedroom. Behind him, the door closed with a soft click. Across the room, her breath caught in her throat with a similar click.

Master's home...

There was just enough light coming through the window to accentuate her silhouette. And, what a silhouette it was. He stripped off his shirt and tie, unzipped his sodden pants. The rasp of the disengaging teeth pierced the silence.

Almost immediately, pre-cum was weeping from his cock in threads. He took hold of the thick root. It pulsated in his palm, primed and ready.

Cock in hand, he advanced towards the bed where Missy lay face down, butt-plugged arse arced high in the air...

Chapter 26

The king-sized bed dipped with his weight.

Other than one seemingly endless tremor, Missy remained motionless. Her pelvis rested atop three firm pillows. Her breasts, squashed against the mattress, bulged from both sides of her rib cage. Her head was turned towards the bedside table where her collar sat. Her lips were parted, her breath fast and shallow.

To James, she was the embodiment of female perfection.

On his knees between hers, he could just make out the tips of two slimy fingers jiggering between her legs. Creamy cunt juice coated both of her inner thighs. The top pillow was soaked. He admired the heart shaped ass spread wide before him. Smack dab in the middle sparkled the crown jewel of the butt-plug. The faux-ruby winked at him, an irresistible invitation. James grinned, tipping his head in gracious acceptance.

His cock was throbbing. If his scrotum were any tighter, his balls would explode.

Enough is enough!

In rapid succession, he dealt three sharp smacks to each unblemished buttock. In the pronounced silence, they cracked like gunfire. The most adorable squeals followed each blow and preceded the next. Before the two crimson flowers were fully bloomed on her ass, he draped his body over hers. Skin to skin, her flesh scorched his. His cock was glued to her dripping slit.

James kissed and nibbled the entire column of her neck from shoulder to hairline, inhaling her essence. Her shiver turned into moaning convulsions. When he reached her ear, he tongued it inside and out before whispering into it.

"Master adores his dripping whore."

The shock wave that coursed through her body might have dethroned a smaller man. James, however, had no trouble keeping his seat atop his thrashing filly. She was ready to be mounted. It was his pleasure to accommodate.

Repositioning himself between her legs, he took a firm grip of the butt-plug. With no further ado, he unscrewed it from the dark orifice. It released with a sensual little 'pop'. Her accompanying grunt did nothing to assuage his desire. Much the opposite, in fact.

He lined up the mushroom head of his dick with her loosened hole and grabbed hold of her hips. She shrieked with the first probing thrust, her skin clammy with perspiration. James paused, giving her time to adapt to the breach. The sensation of her violated anus convulsing around the head of his cock was sheer heaven.

"There's my good girl. Master knows what his little one needs. He knows how much you like your pretty little ass fucked, don't you, baby?"

There was no verbal response. Instead, Missy's 'pretty little ass' spoke on her behalf. It squeezed his dick as though all life on earth was dependent upon it. To the true submissive, giving of herself anally was an almost religious experience. The pain, the taboo, and the knowledge that she was pleasing the man she worshipped was an irresistible trifecta that led straight to sub-space. James cooed to her, stroking her sweat-slick flank.

With no effort whatsoever on his part, she worked his cock into her deepest and darkest crevices. The effect was immediate.

"Rub that fat clit, whore. I'm going to blow a load so far up your ass you're going to taste it!"

And with that, he let loose. Past the point of no return, he sawed into her. With each thrust, she bucked back against him, bringing them closer and closer to the edge.

Somehow, Missy got there first. He held tight to her grinding hips as she squirted all over his ballsac. She moaned through the entirety of her orgasm, her rosy bottom locked onto his phallus. He gritted his teeth until she was spent, her mind and body nothing more than a quivering mass of nerve endings.

James roared, abandoning all control. This was the perfect union of two imperfect souls, and from it he milked every drop of pleasure. Missy's exhausted body flopped helplessly beneath him as he pounded his seed into her bowels. It was seconds, minutes—perhaps even eternities before his orgasm began to recede.

All that was left was their staggered breathing and the sharp tang of anal sex. James blanketed her body with his, both shuddering in the aftermath. The convulsing communion of mind and body was nothing short of dazzling. It was some time before he was able to muster the wherewithal to remove the pillows from under her hips and gather her into his arms.

Laying beside her, he pulled her leaking bottom tight against him, spoon style. One arm encircled her waist, holding her close. The other supported her head, his hand reaching around to gently cup her breast. James buried his face in the hollow between her shoulder and neck. Her pulse thrummed against his lips.

Kissing his way up to her ear, he tongued it inside and out before whispering into it.

"Master loves his precious whore..."

Chapter 27

Missy felt like a princess.

The shiny Volvo SUV was fully loaded with built-in...*everything.* The number of country music stations alone was staggering. She flipped through them, her hand never leaving the leather-wrapped steering wheel. The ride was so smooth, she'd swear the tires weren't touch the road.

The on-board GPS indicated that she was over halfway there. She sat tall in the drivers seat, albeit shifting from butt cheek to butt cheek. Each time she re-adjusted her position, she flushed. It was one thing to engage in anal sex. To squirt all over the room while doing so was quite another.

"Master loves his precious whore."

Missy shrugged, finding serenity. Serenity mixed with a healthy dollop of pride, to be honest. Offering herself in such a manner was the epitome of submissiveness—an honor to give, a gift to share. Her reaching orgasm during the socially abhorrent act was simply a...tribute. A testament to their bond.

"Take exit ramp I-18. One third mile."

The confident, seductive voice of the GPS spoke, and Missy paid close attention.

James refused to let her drive her ancient car on the highway. She'd been moved to tears when he gifted her with Angeline's vehicle, which he'd kept immaculate for the three years since her death. A tune-up and quick rinse later, and it sat sparking in the driveway, filled with gas and gifts for Christopher.

At the last moment James added a stunning Tag Heuer timepiece. After seven years at Boutique Ebony & Ivory, Missy knew a thing or two about watches. It was overwhelming, really. This man's keen interest in her son meant the world to her.

He may prefer a game of go fetch to a game of go fish, but he loved fearlessly and with his whole heart. He'd laughed when she fawned over it, joking that it was for Christopher, not her.

Laughing with him, she'd thrown her arms around his neck. James bent, kissing the top of her head. She felt the heat of him as he pressed her against the car. He cradled her head and kissed her for real. His lips were sweeter than cotton candy. She melted into him, prolonging the moment.

It was James who broke it off, peeling those luscious lips from her greedy mouth. In a flash, he'd opened the driver's door and she'd ducked under his arm to climb aboard. Literally. Once behind the wheel, the seat belt took it upon itself to wrap snugly around her body. She laughed again.

She rolled the window down, reminded him where she was staying and what her plans were with Christopher and company. At the last possible second, she'd handed him the card.

"Have a good weekend, sir. I miss you already."

"Bear right. Take exit ramp I-18. Fifty feet."

Missy was still getting used to the SUV's gizmos and gadgets. Locating the turn signal, she bore right and took exit ramp I-18.

She'd meant to talk to James about Ethan before she left. But, somewhere between the excitement over the new vehicle, getting it loaded, and saying goodbye to the man she adored – it slipped her mind.

"No secrets and no privacy, little one..."

Missy frowned, a twinge of guilt knitting her eyebrows together. All she had was a bad feeling—no hard evidence. On the other hand, something was hinky, she could smell it. Things just didn't add up.

Admittedly, she'd been in a bit of a pea soupy fog after Luke's attack, but that was a week ago. Now, her mind was clear. And troubled. She'd been lulled when Ethan's nasty messages stopped after the initial flurry. She'd minimized them, passing them off as the result of a childish tantrum.

Since then, however, other strange occurrences had begun to niggle. Taken individually they seemed benign. Collectively, they set off alarm bells. That unmarked Hummer with the blacked out windows, for instance.

Had it been following me?

Her gut said yes and Missy always trusted her gut. At the time, she'd put it off to paranoia. Now, she checked her rear view mirror more often.

Then there was Ethan's blue handkerchief. She couldn't get it out of her head. *Did I really miss it the first time back to the house?* It sure caught her attention the second.

Was it even possible...?

On the outskirts of the bustling college town, Missy reduced her speed. She was so excited to see her boy. She did her best to dispel her suspicions, attributing them to the whimsies of a fanciful imagination. After all, what did she think a big shot like Ethan was going to do? Kill her for leaving him in a five star restaurant? Surely, he had bigger fish to fry. It was almost too ridiculous to entertain.

Almost...

She'd discuss it with James the moment she returned. Either she was hallucinating, or there were too many coincidences to be coincidences...

Chapter 28

Again and again, Missy cleared her clogged throat. She was determined not to start bawling like a baby. As it was, silent tears were leaking. Her little boy was all grown up, and yet here he was, unabashedly hugging his mother. For the second time. The first time he'd lifted her clear off the ground.

She held him tight, overcome with joy and pride. How she loved this amazing young man. She may have raised him, but, his very existence had kept her sane.

"Honey, it's just wonderful to see you! Is it possible that you've grown? It's only been a few weeks!"

His roommates, Brendan and Bob, stood off to the side, pink from embarrassment. The three boys were childhood buddies. Shuffling their feet and grinning, the teenagers weren't quite sure what to make of the overt display of emotion from one of their own.

When she'd pulled in, the trio was already galloping down three flights of rickety looking steps to meet her. Her instinct was to call out to them to be careful, but she resisted the temptation. She trusted Christopher's judgment. No doubt, he'd already calculated the maximum rate of descent over the degree of gradient times his physical capability.

Who knew what went on in that brilliant brain of his.

Christopher, or Chip, as his friends called him, was born older than his years. His analytical streak ran deep, curbing any desire for senseless risk taking. As his mom, she was just fine with that.

The boys unloaded the car, making a couple of trips. If she didn't stop them, they'd have ripped open the birthday presents right there in the parking lot. On the other end of the spectrum, the shiny new SUV failed to make any discernible impression. Between the three of them, they'd managed to come up with a single tepid remark.

"Nice Volvo, mom."

And then it hit her. Amongst the packages was a tube filled with posters that she'd taken off his bedroom walls. They were a collection of hot girls and even hotter cars. Missy called out to their retreating backs.

"What would you have preferred boys? An Aston Martin?"

Their heads almost spun off their shoulders. The flabbergasted looks they shot her were comical. *What could a mother know of such things?* Chuckling, she followed them up to their little apartment. She wasn't surprise when the stairs weren't nearly as rickety as they'd appeared.

The little apartment, however, was in dire need of some good old-fashioned motherly love. A one-bedroom unit, its contents consisted of one box-spring and mattress. Two other mattresses, including Christopher's, were on the floor in the main room. Wooden crates served as both tables and chairs.

'Devices' cluttered every surface: computers, phones, headphones, game units and more. Music was coming from somewhere. She had no idea from where.

It was obvious they'd attempted a last minute clean-up. Emphasis on attempted. She shook her head at the mountain of pizza boxes and bags of empty soda cans next to the door. Setting the birthday cake on the counter, she turned to the boys.

"Who's hungry?"

She wasn't surprised by the unanimous response. The still-growing boys weren't just hungry, they were, by all accounts - 'starving to death'.

"Let's deal with this stuff later, kids."

Besides gifts, she'd brought end tables and lamps, dishes, bedding, pots and pans and some much needed cutlery.

"What's the best restaurant in town? It's time to celebrate!"

Chapter 29

Ethan was horny.

Clearing his office mid-meeting, he made himself comfy on one of the three vacated sofas and pulled a raging boner out of his pants. His crew was used to his abrupt schedule changes, not to mention his indifference to the chaos they created.

This was Ethan's world. Everyone else simply inhabited it, pawns to be used and abused.

He was peripherally aware of his narcissism thanks to his drunken mother. Unfortunately, other than hurling profanities that would make a sailor blush, she did nothing to tame the burgeoning beast. In fact, she fueled it.

Growing up, young Ethan engaged in what was his father brushed off as 'boyish pranks'. These so-called pranks escalated from bullying and window peeping to fraud and assault. Lucky for him, his powerful father was many things, including an indulger of children.

An indulger of his child, at least.

Ethan Montgomery II pulled every string at his disposal to keep his boy out of juvie and then out of jail. He called in long-forgotten favors, no matter how minuscule. He never balked when threats and intimidation were required. Palms on both sides of the law were generously greased. In short, he did whatever it took to keep his spoiled, wayward son consequence free.

Only one misguided judge stuck to his bleeding-heart convictions. The all-too-honorable George T. Weatherly refused to partake of the kool-aid, no matter how much sugar was added. Ethan was seventeen, caught yanking off in public. Again. His anger swelled and his cock shriveled in his hand at the injustice he was forced to endure at that tender age.

After all, he hadn't been 'in public', he'd been well hidden behind tall bushes. And, how was he supposed to know he was right in front of some cunt's bedroom window? His father was beside himself when Weatherly took her word over his sanctified son's.

At least he'd been a juvenile. They'd been able to get the charges reduced and the record sealed, never to see the light of day. Nonetheless, he'd sworn to remember the goody-two-shoes adjudicator that nearly succeeded in besmirching his family name.

Twenty-five years later, he didn't recognize the old man until Missy introduced them at The Pitts. Twenty-five years wiser, Ethan knew enough to not ruffle his incorruptible feathers. He preferred to deal with more malleable types. Dumb sluts like Missy Weaver, for instance.

Speaking of the dumb slut, Ethan hoarked deep in his throat then spit the ball of phlegm into his palm. Coating his drooping cock, he jerked it to attention, then hoarked and spat again. Lubricated to his satisfaction, he closed his eyes.

Try as he might, Ethan couldn't maintain a hard-on. Every time he envisioned Missy astride his cock, it withered to nothing. Frustrated, Ethan reached for his phone and tapped 'Video'. Finding what he needed, he held the phone steady in one hand and pulled his already stiffening pud with the other.

This particular video was taken months ago, yet, it never got old. The image was sharp, the audio clear as a bell. Strung from the rafters by his shackled wrists, a hood covered his head and a metal cage ensnared his tortured genitals. Watching the scene unfold for the umpteenth time, his pulse quickened.

While his breathing escalated as he watched, it wasn't close to the ragged gasps that the actual whipping evoked. Eyes glued to the tiny screen, Ethan lessened the pressure to his cock.

This agony was too sweet to rush...

Chapter 30

Mistress Nevaeh Starr was never more breathtaking than when she was wielding a bullwhip. Her dread-locked hair flew with each snap of the leather-bound handle. Her mammoth breasts quaked with each precision placed strike.

Ethan smirked, remembering the shock and distaste on Missy's face after getting an eyeful of the imposing, cool-as-a-cucumber Mistress. Although not a term he favored, it'd been truly priceless. While he'd been taken aback by her show of bravado, his wish was for the two women to meet again in a much more private setting.

Ethan's wishes always came true. He made sure of it.

On the video, Nevaeh Starr was tormenting the shackled figure with the painfully confined stiffy. Her cold, taunting voice never failed to arouse.

"You're a bad, bad, boy, aren't you Ethan? You know what you deserve. Tell Mistress what a bad boy you are. Beg me to punish you and your pathetic little dick"

Ethan watched dry-mouthed as he did precisely that. He begged and he whimpered from under the leather hood. And, just when he thought he couldn't endure another stroke, he begged and he whimpered some more.

Pleeease, Mistress, pleeeease!

Ethan accepted that even amongst deviants, he was deviant. He was that rare, inexplicable mix of sadist *and* masochist. While he got off on inflicting pain and humiliation on others, he hungered for it, as well.

In the controlled environ of his choosing, of course.

It was an itch that wouldn't go away and refused to be ignored. Years ago in a self-indulgent frenzy, he'd struck paydirt – otherwise known as Mistress Nevaeh Starr. Her impressive collection of whips and canes soothed the beast within, if only for a time.

Such a loyal client was he that she'd captured his likeness on canvas. Mistress might not be as proficient with a paintbrush as with a cat-o-nine-tails, but she wasn't too shabby, either. Hooded and hanging, his portrait held a place of honor on her waiting room wall.

At the two minute, twelve second mark, the video reached its apex – Ethan's cue to increase the pressure to his cock. Nevaeh Starr was advancing on his unsuspecting form. Breathing hard from the exertion of wielding the whip, she stood directly in front of his writhing and helpless body. Viciously, she twisted his nipples as she cooed into his veiled face.

"I bet naughty little Ethan wants to come, doesn't he? Let's see what we can do about that, shall we?"

'Naughty' Ethan had this timed down to the second. He could almost feel the sweat pouring down his face under the heavy leather hood. In the video, two of her inch-long claws were working their way between the bars of his cock-cage. In real time, he abused his genitalia, wrenching at his dick with brutal abandon.

Mistress' sharp nails scraped at his pebbled scrotum, leaving marks that stung for days. There was no forgetting the red-hot ecstasy as his tortured balls prepared to deliver their load. It was then that another of those razor-tipped weapons violated his asshole. Buried to the hilt, it squiggled around like a rabid gerbil. His imprisoned cock strained to reach orgasm, yet was unable to achieve full extension. Nonetheless, his jism oozed in globules down his bent dick and onto the floor.

Splayed on the creamy leather sofa in his cushy penthouse office, Ethan groaned, erupting in orgasmic unison.

When at last he was freed, his 'Thank you, Mistress!' was a shaky, if enthusiastic, falsetto. To this day, it was unrecognizable to his own ears. The final seconds of the video were winding down, yet Ethan remained glued to the screen, shriveled cock forgotten.

In his heart of hearts, the ending was his favorite part.

He watched as, of his own volition, he got down on his hands and knees. Using only his tongue, he cleaned up his mess...

Chapter 31

James pressed 'End Call' then resisted the urge to throw the phone across the room. To say he was pissed was an understatement. He knew that with Missy away, it wasn't going to be the best weekend on record. But, he didn't expected it to go straight to the crapper, either.

The fat CEO of Shindigo Corporation was requesting a full power-point presentation at their next board meeting. That would be the same CEO who'd assured James that the buck stopped at his desk. Evidently, that wasn't the case when it involved a re-structuring that began with the big boys.

The board convened once a month. This month, the auspicious occasion happened to land on a Monday. *This Monday.*

All things considered, *that* was the good news. He'd just gotten word that Luke Weaver was out on bail. Frankie Shanahan, one of the responding officers at the scene, was kind enough to give him a head's-up. He'd been arraigned and a date was set for trial. But for now, he was walking the streets a free man.

James couldn't imagine who might have sprung him, and Officer Shanahan wasn't privy to the information. He thanked him through gritted teeth, his mind already kicking into overdrive.

He didn't believe for a second that Luke would be *that* stupid twice. He'd seen the terror in his jaundiced eyes, smelled the defeat on his putrid breath. He wouldn't be looking to run into James again any time soon. Not to mention that now, he was outfitted with an electronic ankle bracelet and a restraining order.

Luke was a broken man, as ineffectual as he was pathetic. If James were more empathetic towards losers, abusers, and absentee fathers, he might feel a modicum of sympathy. As it was, he was more concerned with who would go to the trouble and expense of posting his bail. Missy said he'd alienated everyone in his life. Or vice versa.

Speaking of Missy...

Fuck, he missed her. James got up from the desk, gave his head a shake, and went to take a piss. He really needed to pull on some big boy panties. She'd only been gone a day and a half, for god sake. She'd be home tomorrow.

Home?

Yes, home. In his head, the beloved Victorian manse that he'd shared with Angeline was now as much Missy's home as his own. He still felt his deceased wife's presence, but instead of angst, her memory now engendered feelings of warmth and comfort. She approved of Missy. He could feel it.

Years of unfounded guilt had melted away like snow in springtime. James emerged from the terrible darkness of mourning into the blinding beauty of life. And love. In a nano-second, his world went from mind numbing grey to brilliant Technicolor. He grinned. The future was so bright, he needed sunglasses.

Fully clothed, he stretched out on the unmade bed. Missy was everywhere. Her hair was on the pillows and sheets, as was her sweat and their combined cum. So palpable was her essence that with every inhalation, he could virtually taste her. The intoxicating wench had him at 'hello'. *Before* hello, if he recalled correctly.

Submissive...

James rolled onto his side. A late afternoon siesta was just what the doctor ordered. Missy's framed visage beamed at him from the bedside table. Beside it, her collar. It was a toss-up which sparkled brighter, her eyes or the diamonds embedded in the leather.

He'd added one other item: the card Missy gave him just before she left. James didn't reach for it, there was no need. The poem was committed to memory, if not etched into his soul. His eyes closed as it played in his mind like a lullaby.

"Existing in limbo, no peace in my soul,
Could never confess, yearned a Master's control.
Now where I belong, you help me to heal,
Content at your feet where you taught me to kneel.
Honor in service, strength, courage and grace,
As Yin is to yang, safe in your embrace."

James growled. That collar belonged around her neck as surely as she belonged at his feet as his submissive and at his side as his life partner.

James determined to make that happen upon her return...

Chapter 32

"Suck me off with that sexy voice of yours, little one."

Every word cartwheeled through her brain, causing her ears to ring and the muscles in her lower abdomen to contract. What little breath was left in her body left in a single and sudden whoosh, as though from physical impact. *Wha'?*

There was no doubt that Dominance ran in this man's veins, as vital to his being as oxygen and blood. It wasn't something he played at or dabbled in. He did not pull it on and off like a coat. It was who and what he was from the day he was born.

Master...

From her somewhat contorted position, Missy did her best to comply. Her knees were bent and spread, thighs pulled up so high they rested against her flattened breasts. At the same time, her lower back was arched off the mattress.

One hand was busy between the bloated lips of her sex, triggering orgasms at James' behest. Three fingers of the other hand were tickling her own tonsils, triggering her gag reflex for his auditory enjoyment.

The phone was on the pillow next to her ear, set to 'Speaker'. His breathing became more frenetic as he teetered closer to the brink. In her mind's eye, Missy could see his imposing, vein-riddled cock pulsating in his imposing, vein-riddled hand. After talking her through two screeching orgasms, it was his turn.

A day that began in full 'Mommy' mode was culminating in down and dirty 'submissive' mode. Life was good!

Whereas the night before Christopher slept on the second bed in her hotel room, tonight he'd balked at the suggestion. He was itching to get back to his boys and his toys after another hectic day with mom. She'd chuckled at his honesty. In truth, she sympathized. The quaint hotel room was a welcome oasis after another hectic day with her son.

She felt more at ease about the distance that separated them. She saw that Christopher was in his element, prepared to tackle the challenges of college life. Missy gave herself the proverbial pat on the back. She'd raised a confident, independent young man eager to take on the world.

Proud as she was, she couldn't fathom why a tear rolled down her cheek. A speck of dust, no doubt.

In any case, they were having breakfast together in the morning. She'd saved James' watch as a last minute surprise. School started on Thursday. Knowing her boy, she had a feeling the tech-y timepiece would be a prominent and permanent accessory.

With the unsolicited aid of his roommates, he'd opened the other presents in the apartment. Between herself and three teenage eating machines, there was precious little left of a cake that was meant to serve ten. And, that was *after* an enormous feast at *Hogwarts Off Campus,* a bustling, non-alcoholic 'bar' and grill. At last, she'd put the boys to work, organizing furniture and taking out the trash.

She'd just walked through the hotel room door when her phone pinged. James' timing was perfect. She wasn't surprised.

Now, it was closing in on the witching hour and Missy was a whore possessed. Deep in sub-space, she shuddered in the aftermath of two searing orgasms. Her muscles were the consistency of syrup. The sheet beneath her was tangled, damp from sweat and other unmentionable body fluids.

Suck me off with that sexy voice of yours, little one.

Her voice was strong, if shaky. To her, if sounded like it was coming from another galaxy. For once, she was grateful they were on the phone and not face to face.

"Master, I see you standing before me, muscular legs set wide apart. I kneel up, drooling to take you deep into my throat. I can smell the musk of your balls and want desperately to bury my face into them and lick them clean. I would use such long and loving strokes, sir, the entire length of my greedy tongue. My breath is hot, panting into your groin.

"I so need to taste you, but know better than to take such liberties without your permission."

On the other end, James actually gasped. Even he was shocked by her brazen words. Not shocked to the point of having her stop, mind you. His voice sounded strained, as though it were forced out from between gritted teeth.

"Of course you have my permission, pet. But, not so fast. It is not my wish to come with you suckling at my sac. This load is aimed straight for your belly, and I shan't be pleased if it lands elsewhere. Now, hold the phone to that sloppy hole of yours. I want to hear you finger fucking yourself."

This may be her first phone sex experience, but Missy knew it qualified as a humdinger. The fact that she could be alone in a room, twisted like a pretzel and coming like a whore was in itself astonishing. That she was holding a phone at pelvis height as her fingers plumbed her over flowing pussy was downright inconceivable.

And yet, here she was, humping her hand as though the future of all mankind was hanging in the balance. The obscene sloshing sounds caused her ears to burn. James' delighted murmurs caused her nipples to do the same. The dichotomy had her edging towards an unprecedented third orgasm.

Whore!

When his breathing steadied, Missy took a deep breath and continued. She sensed that James was employing every ounce of self-control that he could muster. It was clear that at this point, there wasn't much left. She got straight to the point.

"When your balls are immaculate, sir, my tongue takes on a life of its own. Shameless in its pursuit, it reaches for...darker realms. It skims the taut, smooth pathway from your scrotum to your asshole. Once there, it laps tentatively, unsure how to proceed."

Missy could not believe what was coming out of her mouth. And still, her pussy swelled, her clit ached.

"There's no mistaking your invitation, sir. What was once tightly puckered relaxes, pressing silent directives against my eager lips. Words are redundant. I am shameless as I lick, suckle, and probe. I resist when, at last, you pull me away."

"I sit back onto my heels, tongue out, face glistening. My hands are clasped behind my head. At your smile of approval, a spurt of viscous pride dribbles freely to the floor. Master's proud little cocksucker. I watch as you feed your hungry whore, stuffing inch after inch of your thick..."

The roar was deafening. In its aftermath, all she heard was the whap, whap, whap of his hand as her reward shot from his balls on the other end of the phone. His breathing was a series of staccato grunts. Missy knew that each marked a volcanic spurt of hot jism.

"Suck it baby. Drink it...all...that's a good girl..."

His words were garbled, guttural. Nonetheless, Missy remained in position, thighs to chest, back arched. In her mind, she was at James' feet with his cock jammed down her throat.

Alone in her hotel room, she swallowed again and again, not wasting a single drop...

Chapter 33

"I love it. *Love* it! I don't even know what to say. I guess thank you is a good start. *Thank you*, Mr. Colton. Did I mention I love it?"

It was rare to see her analytical, even keeled son so animated. Christopher's eyes were about the same size as the stack of syrup-soaked pancakes he'd just inhaled. Huge. He tried to shoot her an accusatory scowl from his side of the table, but it fell well short. The ear-to-ear grin plastered across his face made it impossible.

"Yeah, mom just gave it to me now. She's been holding out all weekend."

Their cutie-patootie waitress stopped by the table, armed with coffee. It was one of the few times Christopher tore his attention away from the sleek accessory already strapped to his arm. As she refilled Missy's mug, the teenagers did what teenagers are wont to do: they gave each other the once over, avoiding eye contact at all costs.

Ah, well. Maybe they'll work up the nerve to text one day.

Missy half-smiled at the intersection of technology and hormones and sipped her second cup of coffee. Her stomach was bulging, having done okay in the eating department herself. If she learned anything last night, it was that phone sex built up one hell of an appetite. In one gulp, she swallowed her coffee, her laughter, and her inappropriate thoughts. This was neither the time nor the place for such musings.

She tuned in to Christopher's end of the conversation. Listening, her heart swelled with emotion. The son she adored approved of the man she worshipped, and vice versa. The relationship that was blossoming between the two of them gave her a sense of completion she hadn't known was possible. This was her family, small yet perfect. Just what she'd always wanted.

"That sounds awesome, Mr. Colton. I mean James. I'll keep you posted and I'll see you on Thanksgiving."

Christopher thanked him again before saying goodbye and disconnecting the call. There was a strange look on his face as he passed her phone across the table.

"I don't know why, but for some reason it just feels wrong to call him James."

Missy tucked the phone into her purse, hiding the surprise that must be written all over her face. *He felt it too.* She made no response, just nodded in understanding. It felt wrong when she called him James, as well.

Master...

She paid for breakfast, leaving a nice tip for cutie-patootie. It wasn't easy saying goodbye to Christopher, but it wasn't as heart wrenching as the first time. She was his mom, she would never stop missing him. But it was his time to soar and she'd done all she could to ensure his parachute was properly packed. She left him in front of his building with a hug and a reminder to call. Often. He waved all the way up three flights of surprisingly sturdy stairs. Missy sighed, watching until he was out of sight. It was time to go home.

Glancing at the computerized console, she decided to fill up before hitting the road. Finding a gas station on the outskirts of town was simple enough. Unlocking the door to the gas tank was another story. She searched high and low for the release button. At last, the chuckling attendant reached in through the window and located it by feel alone.

Missy laughed, too relieved to be embarrassed. She stuck her head out the window, about to explain that she wasn't dumb, she was just new.

That's when she saw it. The words died in her throat as the back end of what looked to be a beige Hummer disappeared around the corner...

Chapter 34

James woke mentally refreshed. Physically? Not so much. He was in desperate need of the shower he'd been too drained to take the night before. Emphasis on drained. Now, the hair on his balls and his belly were gooey with congealed cum.

He grinned despite the mess, or perhaps because of it. Stretching sluggish muscles, James postponed the shower yet again. Instead, he immersed himself in scalding memories from the previous night. Awash on a wave of contentment, he was flabbergasted when his withered cock twitched. Friction burnt and pretty much glued to his groin, he couldn't manage a piss hard-on just moments ago.

He might be a scoundrel, but he was a one woman scoundrel. There were three years of celibacy to make up for, and according to his rough calculations, that would take the rest of his days on this earth and any future lives, inclusive.

Now, where was I?

Ah, yes. That incredible woman and her filthy whore mouth. James couldn't wait to kiss that mouth, tongue that mouth, possess that mouth as it was meant to be possessed. Without bothering to lift the covers, James scratched his soggy balls.

Like most males, he preferred the visual, the tactile. He was surprised when Missy was able to get him off with words alone. Surprised, not shocked. He'd recognized her true nature the second it blipped on his radar. An x-ray wasn't as transparent.

Nonetheless, she'd come a long way along the road of self-acceptance. In fact, last night had been a lesson in self control – *his!* He'd been hard pressed to hold off longer than a virgin at an orgy. As far as he was concerned, her words were a direct pathway to her wishes. James determined to have her hot little tongue where it yearned to be in the not too distant future. It was the least he could do.

His cock lurched in agreement, inflated to the point of separating from his matted pubes to press against the duvet. James laughed, amazed. Playfully, he eyed the tented linens and had a word with his offending member.

"Are you trying to kill me? Do I look eighteen to you?"

Chuckling still, he checked the time, peeled back the covers, and dragged his lazy ass out of bed. It would appear he'd gone from workaholic to horny slacker in record breaking time.

The thing was, he didn't have to work. Between a stellar career and his parent's estate, James could maintain his current lifestyle well into the next century. Then there was Angeline's life insurance. He didn't need it nor want it, but, nonetheless, he got it. Blood money to his way of thinking.

Work had been his life line after her death. He'd been a machine: eat, sleep, shit, work, repeat. He'd gone through the motions in a pea soup fog of guilt and loss. In the end, he'd come out looking like a hero, professionally speaking. He won every award, hit every milestone, and set new standards that to this day have never been matched.

With Missy in his life, however, his priorities were shifting. He felt alive, a phoenix rising from the ashes of sudden and tragic death. He wanted to live with her, love with her, grow old with her. He wanted to show her the world. Last but not least, he wanted to see her fat with his child.

Taken aback by the ferocity of his feelings, James busied himself with pulling on a robe and mentally organizing his day. Removing his phone from its charger, he called his assistant. He considered himself a man of high principles and a professional. There were big contracts in play and he wasn't about to shirk his responsibilities. Once these loose ends were tied up he would implement changes.

"Michael, my main man, I'm in a bind on this Shindigo deal. It's exploded and there's bullshit everywhere. I know it's Sunday, but can you spare an hour?"

With that arranged, there was one more call to make. Missy deserved more than a belly full of imaginary jism and a promise to ream his asshole. He headed for the bathroom, scrolling through his multitude of contacts. He pissed girl-style, still scrolling. At last, he found the elusive number. He wasn't sure she'd answer on a Sunday and was pleasantly surprised when she did.

"Good morning, Teresa, it's James Colton here. I'm wondering, my dear. Do you have any plans for say, early this afternoon?"

Chapter 35

Now in his early forties, Ethan was hailed as a respected pillar of society and a generous philanthropist. His name was splashed across finance and business sections of newspapers on a regular basis. He was also a regular feature on the society page. A financial wizard *and* an eligible bachelor, mothers threw their daughters at him like professional pitchers aiming for the strike zone.

Of course, Ethan was the same law-disabling scoundrel he'd always been. The difference was that, now, he'd sharpened his game, perfected his patter, and upped the stakes. These days he plied his nefarious trades so far beneath the radar, they were virtually undetectable. His motto was that if a tree falls in the forest and nobody hears it? *Who gives a flying fuck?*

This grasshopper had grown more devious and more dangerous than the Master could ever have imagined. Having gotten away with everything short of murder, he believed himself untouchable. The moment that Daddy's intervention was no longer required, neither was Daddy. Long ago, Ethan wrested power of attorney from his feebled hands.

After his mother died from cirrhosis of the liver, or as the obituary called it – *pneumonia*—he had his father installed in an assisted living facility. Not the finest one in town, perhaps, but respectable enough to not raise eyebrows. There, the old man would languish until the cancer finished him off.

According to the nurse who updated him quarterly, he languished still. Long ago, she'd given up urging him to visit his 'poor' father. His only visitors these days were an incontinent sister and their old housekeeper, Birdie. Ethan disposed of used-up people as he did used-up toilet paper: he simply flushed them out of his life.

While it was beneath him, Ethan was driving himself tonight. This was a one-man reconnaissance mission. The fewer cooks in the kitchen, the better. He hadn't been to Montgomery Manor in years, although he paid for its upkeep. From his father's holdings, of course.

His headlights illuminated the long, tree-lined approach. Named in honor of his family's philanthropic ancestry, his mother refused to refer to it as Montgomery Drive. Instead, she dubbed it 'The Green Carpet', a none-too-subtle reference to the Red Carpets of Hollywood. In her vodka-inspired delusions, both led directly to the center of the universe.

He circled the oval track in front of the Tudor style behemoth. What was once alive and lived in was now dark and deserted. The only remnants of its glory days were Birdie Washington, the old housekeeper who still looked after the place, and the gardeners.

Birdie lived on the estate, in a cabin designated for the help. Back in the day, Ethan openly referred to it as the slave's quarters. He still thought of it as such, although he'd learned to keep it to himself. Folks were so sensitive these days. In ay case, the cabin was far removed from the big house by a large expanse of manicured lawns and a thick, almost jungle-like bank of trees. It was accessed from a different road, as well.

The minute daddy dearest died, Birdie would be history. That is, if she didn't croak first. Pushing eighty, she'd dedicated her life to serving generations of Montgomery's. In spite of that, Ethan couldn't wait to boot her leathery ass to the curb. He may not be able to fire her quite yet, but that didn't mean he couldn't relish the day.

The uppity nigger had given him the voodoo stink eye all his life, as if she knew something he didn't. If that weren't enough, years ago she'd lodged some bullshit complaint against him. He'd been enraged when his father chose to remain out of the fray. In the end, he'd hired his own lawyer and settled the matter out of court. He'd also sworn revenge.

All things considered, it could have been worse. Her allegations of racism could have ruined everything he'd worked so hard to attain. And, exposed everything he'd worked so hard to hide. He hadn't forgotten. She'd be out so fast, her head would spin.

Smiling to himself, Ethan made a mental note to notify both Birdie and the gardeners. He was suspending their services for at least a week. It wouldn't do to have them, or anybody else, nosing about.

Ethan peered at the dwelling in which he'd grown up. Dwelling, not home. He'd never thought of it as home. Where the palace-like abode should have appealed to his voracious appetite for excess, somehow, it fell flat. He was devoid of emotion when it came to his parents or anything to do with his childhood. They were the tools he utilized to build his facade. Nothing more.

That's not to say that his parents and their house weren't important to him. They were. After all, they represented his two favorite things in the whole world: Money and power.

His money and *his* power.

He never imagined the place would come in handy. The only reason it wasn't already sold and the money pocketed was because of his father's stubborn refusal to die. Until then, it was difficult if not impossible.

It must have been Kismet, because here it sat, the perfect, sound-proof fortress. Ethan saw no need to enter. Tomorrow, he'd send his most trusted employees to begin installing the specialized equipment.

It was time for his biggest coup yet. Nobody fucked with Ethan Montgomery III and got away with it.

Especially not some worthless, low-life tramp...

Chapter 36

James parked next to Teresa's hundred and fifty thousand dollar Tesla Model S. He gave the sleek vehicle the once over. Twice. *Pretty fucking sexy.* He had to hand it to Teresa. The eccentric woman lived her life loud, proud, and stylin'.

Boutique Ebony&Ivory had the rare distinction of attracting old money and new, young and old alike. A converted 1920's two-story building in the middle of an affluent residential area, it was unique not only in address, but also in inventory and ambiance.

Teresa inherited the business from her mother, then went straight to work on renovating and reinventing. In less than a decade, she'd turned a conservative neighborhood staple into an international fashion mecca to be reckoned with. All credit went to Teresa. She didn't follow trends, she invented them.

James gave her a lot of respect.

He did not, however, find her sexually attractive. He was forced to make that point crystal clear after Angeline's death. As a couple, they'd shopped at Ebony&Ivory where the two women became fast friends. On several occasions, Teresa would join them for dinner or a show.

After Angeline's death, she was quick to commiserate, offering an understanding, if boney, shoulder to lean on. She came by the house to check up on him, laden with baked goods or fresh fruit. He was a mess, a walking zombie, drinking more than thinking.

He should have noticed when she started dropping by empty-handed and dressed to kill, but he didn't. In the vice-like grip of grief and guilt, he'd been oblivious. That is, until the day she wound up in his lap, puckered up and zeroed in. *That* snapped him out of his fog in a hurry. Bolting upright, she'd literally hung from him like a human bib. Small but feisty, her arms were locked and loaded around his neck.

It didn't end well. She'd laughed, but the shrill titter spoke volumes. Teresa was deeply humiliated by his graceless rejection. Needless to say, she never stopped by again.

Fast forward three years. When Missy told him she worked at Ebony&Ivory, his memories of Teresa were fond. As far as he was concerned, the incident was ancient history, water under the bridge. Or...gin, in this case. *That woman could drink an Irish sailor under the table!*

When he dropped by the boutique last spring to visit Missy, he'd wondered how Teresa might react. After all, anything was possible when it came to a woman scorned, and *this* particular woman wasn't exactly bashful. His concerns were without merit. She was her old self - friendly, zany, and more than willing to offer her opinion.

Of course, James was grateful when Teresa agreed to open the store for his convenience. Still, he thought it prudent to err on the side of caution. Under one arm was an enormous box of truffles. *Not* the sort filled with liqueur. He saw no reason to invite trouble, no matter how remote the possibility.

James stepped through the unmarked back door, left open in anticipation of his arrival. It was a decidedly less glamorous entranceway than the story and a half extravaganza around front. Once inside, it was impossible not to recall the last time. His attention was immediately drawn to the two private change rooms. The grin that spread across his face could only be of the wolfish variety.

Visions of a lingerie-clad Missy promenaded through his head, much like she'd promenaded down the catwalk behind that very door. Asking her to put a bounce in her step was a stroke of genius on his part, and he didn't mind saying so himself. The memory of her tits joggling as she'd advanced towards him was spectacular. So spectacular, in fact, that his cock stood up in a show of solidarity.

He adjusted his jeans just in the nick of time.

"James, dah-link! It's simply mah-velous to see you!"

Chapter 37

Teresa pseudo hugged him, faux kissing the air beside each cheek.

That worked well for James. An up close and personal hug at that moment would have given her entirely the wrong impression.

"It's good of you to do this on such short notice, Teresa. I really appreciate it, and you know Missy will too!"

They both laughed, dispelling any residual awkwardness that might have existed. James handed her the chocolates. Teresa grabbed them so fast, he was lucky to get his arm back with the hand attached. Fascinated, he observed as she tore into the box and perused the selection before stuffing two into her mouth.

Complete waste of time having them gift wrapped, that's for sure.

"Sorry, darling, starved. Forgot to eat. In any case, chocolate's the new Cheerios, haven't you heard? Breakfast of champions!"

James laughed again, admiring Teresa's wit as much as her natural ability to put others at ease. As she devoured one truffle after another, he filled the silence.

"You're looking marvelous as usual, my dear."

James wasn't just blowing smoke up her ass, either. Teresa *did* look marvelous, as only Teresa could. Her bleached blonde hair was pinned high on her head in some kind of frizzy french chignon. It being Sunday, she'd toned down her usual blinding attire to the boutique's flagship colors: black and white. Her faux leather leggings bagged on her 'can-never-be-too-skinny' frame. The white camel-hair cardigan? *Stunning!*

"I'm thinking we'll start with that sweater, Teresa, and build from there. That is, if it comes in anything over a size two?"

Oops!

Her head whipped up so fast, he worried she might have self-inflicted whiplash. If looks could kill, it was without a doubt time to kiss his ass goodbye. Her eyes flashed indignation as she masticated the wad of chocolate that bulged in one cheek. She swallowed twice then let him have it.

"I'll have you know this sweater is a size zero. First you steal away my best employee and then you *dare* to insult her ex-boss? You can stick your size two bullshit straight up your size full-of-crap ass!"

While he doubled over with laughter, she made a point of hautily licking every finger clean.

"Now, tell me, lovey. How *is* our girl holding up?"

She might have made a show of turning her back and heading towards the front of the shop, but the concern in her voice trailed in her wake. It was clear that Missy had a true friend and ally in Teresa.

"All things considered, really well. She's a trouper, as you know, tougher than she looks."

James shuddered. A chill ran its course down his spine as it did every time he thought of *that* night. The knowledge of just how close he'd come to losing his kindred spirit tormented still. He forced himself to unclench his jaw. He felt confident that the broken, blubbering Luke was no longer a danger. Yet, something continued to niggle. He was waiting to hear back from George Weatherly. The judge was his best chance of getting the information he needed. He meant to know who sprung Luke. And then, he meant to know why.

Ninety minutes later, Teresa was pseudo hugging and faux kissing him goodbye. The garments he'd selected were wrapped in tissue paper and packed into two E&I shopping bags.

Teresa had punched a code into what turned out to be a vault-like stock room. The lighting was low, but not low enough to obscure the eye-popping contents. He'd ogled the mostly black and white merchandise as Teresa pulled on a pair of light cotton gloves. James thought of Missy's meager wardrobe and his heart swelled. *This is going to be fun!*

"My treat, of course, James."

"Not a hope this side of hell, Teresa."

Their two dominant personalities scuffled for supremacy, at last calling it a draw. James agreed to pay half price. Teresa agreed to let him. With that complex negotiation out of the way, the games began in earnest.

Teresa treated each article of clothing as if it were a wondrous gift from the gods. She didn't touch, she caressed. She spoke of them, or *to* them, with reverence in her voice and passion in her eyes. He trailed behind her, getting a complimentary seminar on fabrics, designers, and overall industry.

He wasn't able to stop the grin that spread unbidden on his face, but he managed to hide it from Teresa. She didn't need to know that his plan was to tear the majority of his purchases from Missy's irresistible body. She'd probably charge him double, or more likely, not sell them to him at all!

Before he'd satisfied his barbarian appetite for short skirts and high heels, James was mindful to select a couple of dresses that would reach below Missy's bruised and battered knees. She was a mature, intelligent woman with a mature, intelligent son. What happened in the Master's chambers would remain in the Master's chambers.

If he had his druthers, he'd attach a leash to her collar and go for a nice stroll, battered knees on full display. But, alas, for reasons he'd never understand, society frowned on such exploits.

James couldn't wait until Missy got home. He wasn't this excited when he gave her Angeline's Volvo. That was just good common sense from his perspective. This was different. He wanted to see her gold-flecked eyes sparkle as she opened each individually wrapped package. More so, he looked forward to the fashion show to follow.

His eyes slid towards the private change area one last time.

He thanked Teresa again and turned to go. His hand was on the doorknob when she called after him.

"By the way, James, darling. Please pass on to Missy that the asshole hasn't been in for over a week. I hope that means he's stopped bothering her?"

A tic began to pulse in his temple. He turned to face her. When he spoke, his voice was dangerously soft.

"Which asshole do you mean, my dear?"

Teresa looked as if she'd just stepped into a giant pile of manure and wished to extricate herself as hygienically as possible. She cleared her throat, stalling for time.

"Ummm...I thought you knew? I was sure you did. Missy said there are no secrets between you..."

She would have babbled on had he not interjected.
"Which asshole do you mean, Teresa?"
"Why, Ethan Montgomery, of course..."

Chapter 38

Missy's jaw began to ache.

On a positive note, it served to distract from the sting of her inflamed buttocks. Scrunched into the miniscule space beneath James' desk, her hands rested on his booted feet, his cock rested on her drooling tongue. It was to remain there for the duration. Soft or hard. No excuses.

At the moment, it was soft.

"What I need, Michael, is a breakdown of expenditure versus expected return based on these sets of criteria."

James leaned forward, no doubt to hand his assistant the 'criteria' to which he was referring. Luckily, she was paying close attention. She tightened her lips around his flaccid shaft and pulled hard to ensure it didn't pop out of her mouth. The chain reaction was immediate.

James responded to the stimuli as men will do when fellated from beneath their desks. Inch by inch, his saliva-drenched member lengthened, working its way down her saliva-clogged throat. She would have pulled back if his hand weren't there to stop her. With a fistful of hair, he held her firmly in place.

In turn, she gurgled at the breach. Saliva poured down her chin whilst other, more gelatinous fluids poured down her thighs.

Whore!

"As you can see, Michael, I tap danced my way through the last meeting. Tomorrow, I need the cold, hard facts."

His next words were spoken with added emphasis on each syllable.

"You know me. I work best from a position of power. I need *all* available intel at my fingertips."

Unbelievable! The man never ceased to amaze. As three and a half inches of his pulsating girth cut off her airway, he spoke fluent 'business' to Michael while at the same time, speaking flawless 'Master' to her. Missy got the point. To say that her homecoming wasn't what she'd envisioned was an understatement larger than the phallus jammed down her throat.

She'd driven home with one eye on the rear view mirror, the other on the speedometer. It'd taken every ounce of restraint to not jam the pedal to the metal and fly to James. The second she arrived, she planned to sit down with him and lay out her suspicions.

Suspicions, my ass.

Today, those suspicions were officially upgraded to fears!

Her attempts to rouse James with the heavy knocker had failed. Very odd, considering his car had been in the drive and the last time they'd communicated, he'd told her how much he was looking forward to her return.

Master misses his precious whore.

For lack of a better option, Missy tried the knob, knowing it was futile even as she reached for it. James had a top notch security system and wasn't afraid to use it. She'd been surprised when the heavy door swung open, more surprised when silence prevailed. She'd called his name.

Nothing.

Ten feet down the hallway, she heard a faint tapping sound. It got louder the closer she got to James' office. Louder still when she entered. James had been sitting at his desk, stone faced. She wasn't able to see his hands, but one booted toe tapped without respite. Her heart rate increased. It thump, thump, thumped in time to his tap, tap, tapping.

As excited as she was to see him, she knew something was terribly wrong. His mono-syllabic greeting confirmed it.

"Come."

Missy didn't hesitate. She covered the distance between them faster than she could say 'I missed you, my Master'. She desperately wanted to throw her arms around his neck, snuggle in his lap, sand share her burden.

She never got the chance. Just as she was about to risk it, his phone jangled. She stood at his side as he took the call. The knot at his jaw spoke to the clench of his teeth.

"Thanks so much, George. It's starting to make some sense, as much as crazy can ever make sense. If possible, I'd like every name, address, phone number, and anything else you can find. Yes, on both of them, and sooner is better. Thanks again, my friend."

When James ended the call, his hand shot out so fast, Missy flinched. It locked vice-like around her wrist as he ground out a single question.

"What haven't you told me about Ethan Montgomery, and why?"

Chapter 39

Missy spilled her guts.

She told him how, in her desolation over their break-up, she'd turned to Ethan. What happened on the couch in her living room. How she'd deserted him at the restaurant after running into James. The goings-on between then and now.

Everything.

She needed him to understand that she hadn't 'kept' anything from him. She'd been traumatized and in her haze, hadn't considered them noteworthy. Now that her mind was clear, the individual, seemingly innocuous incidents added up to trouble.

James' brow remained tight, but his eyes no longer flashed with anger. What remained was an odd mixture of concern and relief. Yes, relief. Missy understood why.

No secrets and no privacy, little one...

He'd forgiven her trespasses once, on the basis of her inexperience. Twice would be seen as an unacceptable breach of trust, an untenable lack of respect. In other words, a deal breaker. Yet, when she'd explained the meandering sequence of events and her state of mind, he was quick to pull her into his lap. She'd nuzzled her head against the hollow of his shoulder. His hand reached up to cradle it.

Master...

At long last, Missy was home.

James spoke with his lips pressed against her forehead. She'd inhaled him into her lungs as though he represented the only oxygen in the universe.

Holding her against him, he'd reassured her that between himself and Judge George, Ethan was a gnat easily quashed. On the other hand, he wasn't about to take any chances. He intended to solicit aid and advice from every available quadrant. Officer Shanahan would be tapped for his expertise. As would a few of James' military buddies.

But, in the meantime...

His fingers tightened against her skull as James helped himself to a fistful of hair. She may have been absolved of guilt, but that didn't mean he was letting her off scot-free.

At the time, she'd been excited at the prospect of being disciplined. She'd panted like a bitch in heat against his throat, nipples stiff through the fabric of her dress. Her panties had been hard pressed to contain her enthusiasm.

Of course, at the time, she'd had no idea what was in store.

Rolling his chair back, James had flipped her over and across his thighs as adroitly as a French chef flipped a crepe. Her overworked and under appreciated panties hadn't stood a chance. The delicate seams yielded with his first persuasive tug.

With both hands on the floor, Missy found herself staring at James' once-tapping boot. Her diaphragm was compressed against his rock hard quadricep, her butt end high in the air. There'd been little time to acclimate to the abrupt change in elevation and scenery. Very soon, other, more 'striking' considerations demanded her attention.

"Just a reminder, little one..."

Missy was never sure which came first: the searing pain or the ear-splitting crack of calloused palm against tender flesh. Not that it mattered. All that mattered was the end result.

Her world had narrowed to the dimensions of James' hand print. She counted fourteen breathtaking strokes and had braced for the fifteenth. She wrapped her arms around his ankle in silent supplication, well on her way to sub-space.

It had taken her a moment to realize that the pounding in her head was in fact the front door knocker.

"You're lucky whore. I was just getting warmed up."

Now, secreted beneath his desk, her jaw was all but paralyzed. She was sure her swollen lips stretched well into the next state, never to return. When James and his assistant were silent, the unmistakable slurping sounds associated with the art of cock sucking filled the room.

She could just imagine the look on Michael's face.

"Alright, then. If we're clear, Michael, I'll be in touch at zero six hundred hours. Would you mind seeing yourself out, my friend? As you can hear, I have some unfinished business that requires my undivided attention."

Missy didn't just blush at his final words, she ignited...

Chapter 40

"Well, hello, Lukie boy. Miss me?"

Luke slumped at his father's decrepit kitchen table, slugging back beer. If James were a betting man, he'd bet that the filthy undershirt was the same one he wore the night he broke into Missy's house and tried to rape her.

Today, the seams were stretched to the absolute breaking point, tighter even than James remembered. A full third of Luke's hairy belly rested on his thighs, exposed. It would seem that being locked up on assault with intent to do harm charges did nothing to dampen his appetite.

Luke was a glowing advertisement for 'three hots and a cot'.

"What da fuck you want? Get da fuck outta here."

Using the back of his hand, James swept Luke's legs from the only other chair, then decided to remain standing. Sitting wasn't worth ruining a perfectly good pair of jeans. Luke's new ankle bracelet clanked when his feet hit the floor. James eyed it, deeming it the perfect accessory for the wife beating creep. It added just the right touch of prison chic.

"I told ya to get da fuck out. I don't remember invitin' you."

Luke slurred like a tough guy, but there was no hiding the tremor in his hands or the spark of fear in his eyes. James' assessment was right on. Here before him sat a broken shell of man. The only threat he posed was to himself and what remained of the beer.

"Aw, Lukie, is that any way to talk to your old buddy? I come all this way to visit, and this is welcome I get?"

James wasn't half as jovial as he pretended. He wasn't here to exchange not-so-clever repartee with an idiot. He was here to find out what the connection was between the idiot and one of the most admired men in town. How did it come to pass that Ethan the Big Shot posted bail for Luke the Loser?

He posed that exact question to the loser in question.

"I dunno why he done it. I never heard of the faggot in my life. You shoulda seen how he dressed, a faggot for sure."

Not only did James refrain from voicing the first response that leaped to mind, he also managed to not reach out and smack the cocksucker upside the head. It wasn't easy. This waste of skin almost cost him Missy. Instead, he forced the corners of his lips upwards into something the inebriated bastard would interpret as a smile.

"Yes, Luke, but what did he want? What did he say?"

Luke's rheumy, piglet eyes squinted at him, assessing. James could almost see his Neanderthal brain cranking into underdrive as he tried to figure all the angles and which would benefit him most. Luke swilled beer, belched, and cracked another.

"I don't know nuthin'. He got me out of jail, gave me a couple bucks, and had his la-de-da chauffeur bring me here while we got 'acquainted'. That's what I know."

There was no trace of the once proud football hero that Missy described. James was prepared for this contingency. Reaching into his pocket, he pulled out a wad of bills. He laid a fifty on the grubby table and slid it towards Luke.

"If you ask me for another penny, this will disappear, no matter where you stuff it. In fact, it will be my greatest pleasure to retrieve it from your gluttonous person. And I promise you, I won't be as gentle as I was the first time."

He relinquished his hold on the bill, keeping his eyes steady on Luke's.

"You remember the first time, don't you, Lukie?"

Luke's already cadaverous skin paled. He didn't touch the fifty. He did, however, start blabbering.

"I remember somethin' now. He wanted to know bout Missy, mostly. You too. Thought him and me'd make some kinda great team or somethin'. He musta re-thunk once I told him I don't know nuthin' bout nuthin'. I was married to the ungrateful cunt, is all. Wasn't really gonna hurt her."

Luke's eyes shifted away.

"Sorry. Anyway, guess I wasn't much help. He kicked me out before the car was even stopped."

"Do you remember what kind of car, Luke?"

Luke snorted, chugging back the remainder of his most recent beer.

"Course I remember. Cars are my specialty."

And with that, he seemed to think the interview concluded. He hefted his weight onto one butt-cheek and slid the fifty into his back pocket. *Fucking moron!* James did his best imitation of a patient man.

"Luke, what kind of car was it?"

"Oh. It was one of them gas-sucking Hummer four-by-four's. First edition. Shit brown. Big Man must have a real little cock or somethin'."

James was out the door before Luke stopped cackling...

Chapter 41

"But, if she wasn't with James, she had to be with my George!"

Stephanie's voice was on the verge of hysteria. She'd put two and two together and was having a terrible time accepting four as the answer.

Missy was multi-tasking. Her phone was tucked under her chin as she commiserated with her friend and attempted to prepare a meal in James' cavernous kitchen. It was a far cry from her postage stamp galley where she could reach every corner without taking a step. She didn't miss it. It had nothing to do with size.

Master...

Three gloriously uneventful weeks had passed since the weekend she'd visited Christopher. While she and James were both cautiously optimistic that life was getting back to normal, she was the more optimistic. He was the more cautious.

Police cruisers still made frequent appearances, silently patrolling the property. She wasn't to go to her house under any circumstances. It too was being patrolled. She still didn't go out without James or somebody James-approved. He continued to have long, serious conversations with George Weatherly, the police, and an old military buddy named Bull.

And, yet, amidst all the hullabaloo, Missy never felt safe. Decades of self doubt, of isolation, and of anxiety were so far in the past, she barely remembered them. She was strong and confident, loved and in love. She'd even gained some weight back and was working out in James' home gym. Sometimes he would join her. Sometimes he preferred to watch. Either way, his presence energized her and made her soul hum with happiness.

Missy kicked her selfish ass back to the present, then kicked it again for good measure. Her sweet friend Stephanie was inconsolable and it was all her fault. If it weren't for her big mouth, Steph would be none the wiser and more the happier. Missy decided that in some cases – ignorance *was* bliss!

Her detailed account of running into James, George, and the cheap floozy at The Pitts had been gnawing at Stephanie since their get together at the country club. It had taken this long to raise her head from the cozy cushion of denial and face the cold, hard facts. Those facts had shocked her to the core. And had galvanized her into action.

"He tells me he loves me every single day, and every single day—I believe him!"

She and the not-so-good adjudicator were married for over thirty years, she'd thought happily. Nonetheless, she had no intention of sticking around if he insisted on behaving in such a tawdry manner. On the other hand, she wasn't about to walk away without one hell of a fight.

"Steph, maybe there's another explanation?"

Steph would have none of it. She was focused on one thing and one thing only: getting her man back. Missy had never seen her easygoing friend so resolute. She promised to do everything she could to help.

They came up with a thirty-day plan which would include an aggressive head-to-toe makeover. It would hit all the high notes: gym, diet, a hot new wardrobe and a sexy new 'do. The works. Of course, the first step was to recruit Teresa. She may be off the wall when it came to her own fashion choices, but when it came to others, her expertise was legendary.

With that general framework in place, there was one last subject to broach.

"How's the sex, Steph?"

The silence on the other end of the phone spoke volumes. Missy was right. There *was* an explanation why George would stray, and it was nothing to do with not loving his wife.

"Steph. He's a man. A make-over's great, but if you'll forgive me for saying so, dear? All George really wants is a blow job."

Chapter 42

"Dinner is served, sir. Please take your place at the head of the table."

Missy tied a clean apron around her waist. The rest of her serving ensemble consisted of one silver heart pendant, one pair of sky-high stilettos, and one nervous grin. And, oh, yes, gobs of candy-apple-red lip gloss.

James was right. She truly was his whore, wanton to the core. Six months ago, she would never have imagined herself with dinner in one hand and a spatula in the other, naked as a jaybird and horny as a toad. Her inner thighs, however, bore the irrefutable evidence of truth. Both were sticky with nature's own lubricant, which poured from her body like water from a broken tap.

It was the spatula that started it, of course. The spatula that started it all, really.

Missy's original plan for the evening was the epitome of innocence. It consisted of dazzling James with her culinary prowess and then, maybe a movie. Yet, the moment her eyes fell on that infernal spatula, her agenda escalated – or devolved, into something quite different.

Her mind did an immediate back flip. It was as though she were standing on James' doorstep that very first night, his virile frame filling the doorway and emptying her lungs. She would never forget the feeling of his fingers as they closed around her throat. Using that anchor, he'd drawn her into his home and into her destiny. He'd spat into her eager mouth - a gift shared between them as his lips took ownership of hers for the first time.

And then there was the spatula. Always the spatula.

She'd chosen the instrument herself, knowing full well the consequences of her actions. He'd made his intentions clear. Nonetheless, she'd presented it to him with pride, hoping he'd be pleased with the selection. He was. So much so, in fact, that he helped her to 'mount' an angled ironing board, kissed her on the forehead – and used it to go to work on her lily-white ass.

That was her first visit to sub-space. Or, as she preferred to call it: sweet heaven on earth.

Submissive...

Yet, despite the profound distraction of the spatula, Missy managed to quell her friend's fears, bake a lasagna, toss a salad, and open a bottle of wine. Two places were set at the massive oak dining table. A pair of tapered candles were burning. She was butt-spanking naked.

Both dinner – and dessert—were hot and ready for consumption.

James was already seated, having read the note she'd taped to the front door. She could hear him humming, just as he'd hummed while delivering thirteen strokes with the spatula. Missy smoothed the poor excuse for an apron over her pubic mound and took a deep breath.

Her heart was pounding so hard, she was sure it was visible through her chest. Her nipples were stiff enough to cut glass. Missy longed for her collar. She literally felt naked without it. Straightening her shoulders, Missy lifted her chin and thrust her chest forward. Balanced precariously on five-inch heels, she wobbled her way into the dining room.

"Dinner is served, sir...

Chapter 43

Fuck, she looks good enough to eat!

James ogled her from head to toe as she teetered towards him. Her teardrop titties bounced this way and that. He saw no reason to disguise his appreciation. He did, however, worry for the fate of the poor lasagna. He was starving. Lasagna would make the perfect appetizer.

What a pleasant surprise it was to find Missy's note taped to the door. After a harried day at the office, he didn't feel much like going out. He far preferred a pre-dinner glass of wine in the comfort of his own home where he could relax, smoke a cigar, and count his many blessings. His little one cavorting half-naked, for instance.

"How was your day, sir?"

"Dull, my darling. Until now."

Missy beamed, setting the lasagna on the table. Miraculously, it was still in one piece. James nabbed the frilly hem of the blink-and-you-missed-it apron, lifting it just enough to feast his eyes on what lay beneath. Missy dropped the spatula, startled.

"Be still, whore. You know it would be my pleasure to turn you over my knee and use that on your glorious behind. If you recall, the first time did wonders for your disposition."

Missy's compliance was immediate, her cheeks flushing as red as her lips. Or, as red as her ass after a nice session with the spatula.

"Did you really think this scrap of fluff was going to protect you? In fact, why am I doing all the work? Hold this up so your Master can get a better look."

He couldn't help but smile when she used both trembling hands to execute the simple task. The cock-teasing noises she emitted defied description. They culminated in an encore worthy composition of squeaking, squawking, and squealing. All of a sudden, James' custom-tailored pants were pulling in all the wrong places.

He leaned back, relieving some, but not nearly enough pressure. Without taking his eyes from her oozing gash, he unclasped his pants and unfurled his cramped genitalia. Using his cock as a pointer, he addressed her sopping thighs.

"Perhaps a diaper might have been the more prudent choice?"

This time, there was no mistaking the horrified gasp. James chuckled, pulling her onto his lap before she fainted. His cock found its way between her ass cheeks as if magnetically drawn.

"You look especially fetching this evening, little one."

She turned to smile at him over her shoulder. Her goopy grin lit up the room and melted his heart. He reached around to cup both breasts, each a perfect handful. Pulling her tight against him, he inhaled her scent and exhaled the stress of the day. Feather kissing her throat from shoulder to hairline, he breathed into her ear.

"It's hard to say which smells more appetizing, my whore or her lasagna."

Missy's laugh was easy on the ears and contagious. She wriggled her bottom against him, securing his member in the dark chasm. She contracted her strong gluteal muscles, in effect 'hugging' his cock again and again.

Oh! And again.

Life didn't get any better than this...

Chapter 44

Or, did it?

Dessert was even more delectable than the main course. And, that was saying something. Missy's lasagna was one of the best he'd tasted.

The pan was pretty much empty, if you didn't count Missy's hair. He'd 'neglected to move it when he scooped her up and laid her on the table. She would need a shower when he was done with her, of that there was no doubt.

He was a far cry from being done with her, however. At the moment, her ass was hanging over the edge of the table, cunt glistening in the candlelight. A dainty ankle rested on each of his shoulders, stirrup style. Had he a speculum, he'd have performed the BDSM version of a pap smear.

But, alas, all he had was his tongue.

His tongue and a quart of vanilla ice cream, much of which was dripping down her slit, and, as a direct result, off his chin. James grinned. Missy wasn't the only one who needed a shower.

He buried his face in her swollen sex, partaking of the creamy stream once again. After some zealous experimentation, he'd learned that a scoop of ice cream applied directly to the clitoris extinguished any hope of achieving orgasm. He'd tested and proven the theory's veracity more than once now.

From his vantage point between her legs, he licked his way up her belly. He didn't forget the faint stretch marks above her pubic bone, either. Instead, he paid them particular attention, mindful to kiss each one in tribute to womanhood and motherhood. Missy embodied both, and he adored every inch of her.

He plopped a dollop of ice cream onto each bulbous nipple, squashed them together and shoved both in his mouth. His greedy slurping almost drowned out her rebuttal. The melodious aria came to a halt, replaced instead by one long, luscious moan. Her head thrashed from side to side, auburn tresses sopped in lasagna drippings.

Deep in sub-space, acquiescence oozed from her every pore. The timing was perfect. James relinquished his tittie sundae and stood. He helped Missy into a sitting position at the edge of the table.

"Wait here, my lovely."

He didn't bother to tuck in his rampant erection. He made the round trip to the bedroom and back with it bobbing before him like a metal detector on steroids. But, it wasn't metal he was after. It was leather. And, he knew precisely where to find it.

He removed the diamond studded collar from the box it had languished in for far too long. After the catastrophic first collaring ceremony, he'd contemplated commissioning a new one. Maybe this one had bad karma. In the end, he'd rejected the notion as ridiculous. There was nothing wrong with the collar. It was perfect. *He* was to blame for that fiasco, not an inanimate object. And, certainly not Missy.

Both were collateral damage as a result of his poor judgment. He should never have collared Missy without first telling her of Angeline and removing her 'shrine' from his bedroom.

This was Missy's collar, irreplaceable. James lifted the symbolic adornment to his face, rubbing the soft underside against his cheek. The scent and feel of top-grade leather did nothing to diminish his still raging hard-on. Grinning, he kicked off his sagging pants and returned to the dining room.

She sat at the table's edge just as he'd left her, back-lit with candlelight. She took his breath away, even covered in lasagna and dripping in ice cream. A natural submissive, it was no surprise that her back was erect, her eyes were cast down, and her legs were parted.

"Eyes up, little one."

When she saw the collar in his outstretched hand, she burst into tears.

"Master! I promise...I've learned...I would never...I so miss..."

He cut her off, understanding every garbled syllable.

"Sssh, baby. It wasn't your fault. We've discussed this many times, have we not?"

It was like the sun breaking through after a nasty storm. Missy's entire face lit up, blinding in its beauty. *Jesus, how he loved this woman.*

"Now, get down on your knees where you belong, whore!"

Chapter 45

The steam was so thick, she couldn't see two inches in front of her face. Not that this presented any sort of problem. The only noteworthy item two inches in front of her face was more cock.

On her knees, James' fingers in her hair were all the direction she required. Sheets of hot water rained down on her, making catching a breath more hit and miss than guarantee. More so due to the fact that she'd just slurped one of James' cum-heavy testes into her mouth and was determined to do the same with the other.

Whore!

She'd resisted taking her collar off to shower. It was just too soon. When James went to remove it, she'd made her move. Ducking under his arm, she'd stood with her back pressed against the bathroom wall, shaking her head in supplication.

No way! No way! No way! She repeated the mantra again and again. Not out loud, of course. That would just be silly. Nevertheless, her body language did not equivocate. Her eyes flashed and her fists clenched, albeit loosely. Her collar was where it belonged for the first time in months. She was not about to relinquish it without a fight.

Well, a skirmish, at least.

His grin said he heard her loud and clear. They played a little game of 'catch me if you can' before he got serious, cornered her, and gathered her into his arms. His eyes sparkled, a billion points of blinding light. *Star-dust? Fairy-dust? Dom-dust?*

No matter. She could die happily lost within them.

Master...

"You win, little one. I, too, prefer it around your neck, where it belongs. We'll loosen it later so it, and *you*, can dry."

He added one sexy sardonic smile to balance the teasing twinkle in his eye.

"Does that meet with your approval, princess?"

Now, with the mosaic of the tile imprinted on her knees, she figured she looked about as princess-y as a drowned rat. A drowned rat with a collar, mind you. Make that a drowned rat with a collar *and* her Master's entire ballsac in her mouth! Yes, with shameless disregard for decorum or propriety, she managed the herculean feat she'd never before accomplished. Missy gave credit to the added impetus of the collar.

Submissive...

James guided her to her feet just in the nick of time, saving her from the distasteful choice of suffocation or drowning. His scrotum, which she'd worked so hard to contain, was wrenched from her mouth without so much as a 'good girl.'

But...when one door closes, another opens. With his hands on her waist, he lifted her into the air. Instinctively, she wrapped her legs around his waist and her arms around his neck.

His face was buried somewhere in her cleavage. Her engorged clit rested squarely atop his accommodating shaft. By her calculations, he'd been hard for hours. Missy availed herself of the opportunity. After all, she'd been denied for those same hours. Bucking her hips, she sought traction where there was none.

As if she weighed nothing, James made his way to a corner of the hexagonal glass enclosure. She looked down, watching as he braced a foot against each wall then tested for stability. She giggled, pulling his face even tighter between her breasts.

"Safety first, sir?"

His response was non-verbal. James pressed her upper body away from his until her back was resting in the corner. At arm's length, she interlaced her slippery fingers around his slippery neck and held on for dear life. This was going to be a bumpy ride. The angle must have been perfect for him because with just the smallest flick of his hips, she was impaled.

Missy grunted at the abrupt and thorough dilation. Eight inches of frustrated manhood pulsed at the center of her being, scorching her soul. There was no sound other than their breathing. If the shower was still running, she was unaware. Unmoving, they panted into the steam that swirled between them, their bodies slick with humidity, sweat, and need.

James leaned forward, sliding his lips against hers.

"You are not to cum before your Master, is that clear?"

While her lips whispered the words 'Yes, sir!', her mind screamed the words 'Yeah, right!' She was so close, a few well-timed kegels would push her over the edge.

Missy was relieved when he began to fuck her in earnest. She rode him, her strong legs locked around his waist, abdominal muscles straining. The race was on, finish line fast approaching. She prayed she could outlast him, but the odds of that were long and bleak. There were certain things she could control and others she was helpless against. James-induced orgasms were at the top of the 'helpless against' list.

She'd gone a lifetime without, save by her own hand. With him, there was no stopping them. Nor did she care to.

"I'm coming!"

Thank god! Missy exploded a nano-second after his howl penetrated her eardrums. Time stood still as each gave and took of the other, becoming one in body, mind and spirit. Flooded, she clenched against his receding member, fighting to keep her Master's seed where it belonged – deep within her. The ecstasy of the moment seemed to last an eternity.

When the crest of the storm passed, their eyes locked in perfect understanding—beacons in the mist to guide each other safely home.

Spoon style, James's arm encircled her waist, holding her close. The other supported her head, his hand reaching around to gently cup her breast. He buried his face in the hollow between her shoulder and neck. Her pulse thrummed against his lips.

Kissing his way up to her ear, he tongued it inside and out before whispering.

"Sweet dreams, little one. Master loves his precious, collared Whore."

Chapter 46

"Hooking hard, my friend."

James shaded his eyes from the late day sun, marking the approximate location of the errant ball. Make that, *another* errant ball. Thus far, George had lost a total of seven Callaway SR1's, and that was assuming this one was retrievable. Considering the cost and caliber of the ball, you'd think it could carry itself to the green.

James chuckled. It sure as hell wasn't the ball's fault. The truth was that George Weatherly was a horrendous golfer. A club looked like an alien object in his hands. His swing was a discombobulated mess, his short game an unmitigated disaster. Watching him golf was like watching a train wreck. For some grotesque reason, it was impossible to look away.

His get-ups were legendary. George took golf's reputation for deplorable fashion to a whole new level. His plus fours would give Payne Stewart a stroke, if he weren't already passed. As it was, he was probably rolling in his grave. In any case, with two holes left to play, James calculated there was enough time left for his atrociously outfitted friend to divest himself of at least two more balls.

It wasn't often they got in a mid-week round of golf. George had called the night before, suggesting the get-together. He hadn't offered any explanation as to why, and James hadn't pressed. His old friend had sounded troubled.

Now, they were both troubled.

"I figured you needed to know, James. Just in case. His name set off warning bells that night at The Pitts, but lots of names do that in my business. When I discovered it was him that paid Luke's bail, I did some digging. It wasn't easy. His records are sealed tighter than Ali Baba's cave."

"The number of offenses he committed as a youth is shocking, their nature even more so. Yet, he suffered zero consequences."

George shrugged, as though the corruption of an entire system rested squarely on his shoulders. He didn't look at James.

"I tried. And I failed. His father was a force to be reckoned with back in the day. There were some mighty powerful folks on his payroll."

James teed off. Squinting, he watched his ball roll to a stop about two hundred and twenty yards down the right side of the fairway. A good, solid drive. He joined George, already in the cart.

"I won't hear of you blaming yourself, George. You did your best in a game with revolving rules. The odds were stacked against you. But, that was then. What do we know about the douchebag now?"

"That's the thing. As an adult, our douchebag looks as clean as the driven snow. And, maybe he is. Remember, what I'm telling you happened a long time ago. He was a teenager. It may be completely irrelevant now, which is why they seal juvie records in the first place."

George's voice became so faint, James wondered if he was thinking out loud.

"Is it possible he just straightened out the day he turned eighteen? We're not talking about stealing bubble gum from the corner store here. I've seen enough to know that where there's smoke, there's usually fire."

James disentangled his legs and climbed out of the cart. Judging the distance to the flag, he chose a seven iron. He took a half hearted practice swing, made a minor adjustment, and addressed the ball. It landed on the fringe of the green, a do-able two-putt for even par.

"Well done, my boy!"

They drove the golf cart into the rough and parked. Both disembarked, heading into the thick bramble. They knew the drill. The hunt for George's seventh ball was on.

The judge had dug up some smoke, alright, albeit from twenty-five years ago. Ethan Montgomery III, today's philanthropic pillar of society, was once a very bad boy who'd exhibited some profoundly disturbing behavior. It indicated a serious problem with, first and foremost, women, and second, authority.

Did he grow out of it?

Based on everything George could find, it appeared that he did. The worst he found was a complaint lodged by a housekeeper years back. Something about racial slurs. But that's where it ended. Nothing more came of it. Other than that, there were a few parking tickets, not a single one outstanding. Not exactly what you'd call hard-core criminal activity. Like George said, Ethan appeared as clean as the driven snow.

Not to mention that in the six weeks since Missy's return from visiting Christopher, there'd been no sign or him. No text messages, no inexplicable happenings, no beige Hummers. Nothing.

It just didn't make sense that he'd risk his entire reputation over a woman he'd dated twice. It made much more sense that he'd recovered from his bruise ego and gotten back to the business of over-inflating his bank accounts.

James threw his clubs in the car and joined George for a sandwich in the clubhouse. Not even seven o'clock and, already, the sun was low on the horizon. Fall was just around the corner. He half-smiled. His old bones would soon be another year older. As usual, there was no discussion regarding the lopsided numbers on the scorecard. The seventh ball was never recovered. Nor the eighth.

"How's Stephanie, George?"

Expecting the usual benign response, James tore into his triple-layer turkey and bacon sandwich. After eighteen holes, he was ravenous. Today, however, George's retort was so far removed from the norm, James choked. The gluttonous hunk of sandwich lodged mid-way down his throat, refusing to budge in either direction.

Eyes bulging, he grabbed for water, more than a little relieved when his throat cleared. That birthday he was dreading a moment ago was suddenly looking pretty damned good! George was still pounding on his back.

"Are you alright, dear boy?"

James gaped at him, tears streaming.

"I'm fine, George. Please repeat what you just said. I'm sure I misheard."

It was George's turn to smile, and his was no half-measure. In fact, it stretched from ear-to-ear.

"I believe you heard just fine, but I'll be happy to repeat myself. What I said was that, last night? Stephanie tried to give me a blow job!"

Chapter 47

"Tried?"

"That's what he said. Tried."

"Did you ask him to um, expand on that, sir?"

"I did not. But, I'm sure Stephanie will fill in the blanks for you, you inquisitive little minx. All George said was that she'd joined a gym, dropped some weight, and looked great. He doesn't know what's gotten into her, but he sure as hell ain't complaining."

Snuggled against his chest, Missy's lips curled into a knowing smile. *Good for Steph!*

James' laughter sounded like rolling thunder. With his arms around her, their feet took on a life of their own, playing an endless game of footsie. She wished they could stay in bed forever. Sadly, that was not the plan. The alarm shattered their sweet dreams more than twenty minutes ago. Now, as she listened to the strong, reassuring beat of his heart, she was overcome with a strange sensation. A random shiver tingled down her spine.

"Don't go, Master."

James pulled her closer. Or tried to. As it was, air would have trouble wedging its way between them. He kissed the top of her head before throwing the covers back. She didn't make it easy for him to extricate himself from her clutches.

"I must go, my little octopus. This is the final meeting with the Shindigo boys. After today, you'll be looking for ways to get rid of me."

She scowled up at him, refuting the ludicrous remark. James scowled back, drew the covers up to her chin and tucked them around her.

"Rest, pet. I need to grab a quick shower. I will not have you worrying about a single thing, do you understand? That's my department. I'll be back in plenty of time to get you wherever you need to go."

He kissed the tip of her nose and was gone. She listened to the faint hiss of the shower, missing him already. A pile of blankets was a sorry substitute for the potent body heat he emitted. Missy stretched, smiling to herself. In her humble opinion, the sun itself was a sorry substitute.

She still wasn't to go anywhere alone, which was fine with her. They may have joked about George's astonishing revelation, but Ethan's antics as a teenager were no laughing matter. She was grateful to be off his radar.

"Kneel up, whore!"

Missy scrambled from beneath the covers. Atop the duvet, she assumed the submissive position that came so easily and felt so right. They'd made sweet, soft love the night before, falling asleep with James spent inside her. Now, in an upright position, his opaque seed streamed from her body. She flushed crimson as it pooled on the quilt between her opened thighs.

James observed, his eyes riveted. Missing nothing, the corners of his sensuous lips lifted. When the gush receded to a drip, he took her chin in his hand and tilted it upward until their eyes met. His were laughing. When he misread the mortification in hers, she was sure it was intentional.

"Awww, don't you fret, my precious. Master will have another load for you very soon."

He ignored her gasp, instead tweaking an unsuspecting nipple before turning away. Missy drank him in with every sense at her disposal. His scent was fresh: a mixture of soap, shaving cream, and toothpaste. Personally, she preferred the smell of his sweaty balls. Nonetheless, this, too, was pleasant.

Whore!

A towel was wrapped around his hips, slung low and slit high. His cock played peek-a-boo with every step he took. Above that were broad expanses of toned, tanned, well-muscled man. *Her* man.

And, just like that, there was a new dampness between her legs. This time, it was all her own. She could tell by the way her clit thrummed and her pelvic muscles spasmed. From beneath tangled lashes she took in James' inadvertent strip-tease. With his back to her, he unknotted the towel and tossed it in the general direction of the bathroom. In Missy's head, the appropriate music cued.

Ba-boomp, ba-boom...

His lats spread like a cape when he bent to pull on low-rise boxer briefs. They, in turn, showcased his lickable backside to a T.

Ba-boomp, ba-boom...

The dress-tease was equally as titillating. Every muscle rippled as he donned a pair of camel colored dress pants and turned to face her.

Ba-boomp, ba-boom...

Choosing a belt from the cherry wood suit stand, James held the flat end against her lips. With the tang of leather in her nostrils, her primal and immediate response was to kiss her Master's belt.

"Good girl!"

Missy sighed a happy sigh as she observed his nimble fingers feed it through the belt loops before reaching for a shirt.

Ba-boomp, Ba-boom...

He looked good enough to eat in a suit, almost as good as he looked out of one. She watched spellbound as he knotted his tie. The normally benign process induced an unfathomable hunger that leeched from the pit of her belly straight to her insatiable pussy.

Ba-boomp, Ba-BOOM!

With a spritz of cologne and a tailored Ted Baker sports jacket, James was the epitome of traditional professionalism. His appearance made it all the more shocking when he nonchalantly buried several fingers inside of her. In a single whoosh, breath and all logical thought were suspended. What remained was the ringing in her ears and the sloshing of her sex.

"My, my. What have we here? A sopping wet cunt. You love it when your Master finger fucks you, don't you whore?"

As he cooed into her perspiring face, his hand consummated the promise of his words. It sliced into her with an expertise that made her dizzy. The fingers of his other hand curled around her collar. With that leverage, he drew her forward until their noses touched.

"Don't you, whore?"

She'd assumed the question rhetorical.

"Yes, sir. I..."

Formulating a proper sentence while his middle finger tormented her G-spot was no simple task. His next request, however, was near-impossible.

"Say it."

Missy was not at all sure that she could. When James spoke such wanton words, it sent bolts of scalding desire coursing through her veins. He had a Master's degree in transforming vulgarities into terms of endearment. It was as magical as Rumplestiltskin turning straw into gold. Yet, the idea of uttering those same words while eyeball to eyeball with James was an appalling prospect, indeed.

"Say it for Master."

And, really, it was just that simple. Her mouth was already gaping. All she needed to do was formulate the words. Her voice sounded raspy in her ears, barely a whisper.

"I love...when Master...finger fucks his whore."

"I'm proud of you, baby. Now, again. Louder this time."

With the mental power exchange complete, Missy found herself deep in sub-space. Everything softened, inhibitions fell away. She gave herself wholly to the man and Master she worshipped. Unrestrained, her hips pumped flagrantly back against his hand as the orgasm built to a crescendo. Sweat poured from her as his fingers worked their magic in her body and his words worked their magic in her mind.

From somewhere outside of herself, Missy heard the screaming.

"Fuck me Master. Please please fuck me hard. I'm coming..."

Chapter 48

She was late. *Again.*

Missy parked the Volvo underground. Using the connecting passageways, she walked the remaining distance to the hotel. She felt anxious. The day hadn't gone at all as planned.

Before leaving, James removed the leather collar and replaced it with the silver chain. She'd licked every one of his gooey finger clean; he'd had no intention of washing his hands. At the time, she'd giggled, imagining him in his meeting with the faint scent of cum wafting from him.

Eau de Pusse'?

In any case, she was no longer laughing. He'd known she was meeting Stephanie at the day spa and promised to be back in 'plenty of time' to take her. Yet, 'plenty' had come and gone. As had 'in the nick of'. Missy had been well into 'not a prayer', and, still—no word from James. Her texts went unanswered. Her calls went to voice mail.

She'd had a decision to make...

Rushing into the ladies change rooms, she messaged Steph that she'd arrived. Her lucky friend was just finishing up a relaxation massage that was originally booked for both of them. Disappointed, Missy was all the more aware of her aching muscles as she changed into a bathing suit and found her way to the spa area.

Only at the lip of the mineral pool did she relinquished the fluffy spa-issued robe. It fell to the tiled floor just as she immersed herself in the soothing warmth. From a societal point of view, her knees were a fright. While she considered them a badge of honor, she knew that others, including Steph, would not see them as such. If possible, she hoped to avoid that particular conversation.

She hardly recognized Stephanie. The make-over they talked about less than a month ago was more like a transformation. The fifty-something year old woman strutted with a new, and yes, sexy confidence. Her hair was cut into a modern bob and dyed a rich chocolate brown. It looked smashing against her peaches and cream complexion. Even wrapped head to toe in a bulky robe, her slimmer silhouette was apparent. She glowed from the inside out.

"Oh my god, I'm speechless. You look ten years younger!"

Steph joined her in the pool, beaming at the compliment. They found adjoining jet streams and got comfy on the underwater ledge. Missy turned to face her friend and was surprised to find tears in her ears.

"I owe all of this to you, Missy Weaver. I don't know how I can ever repay you."

Missy opened her mouth to object, only to find her objection overruled. The counselor's wife had learned a thing or two over the years.

"Hush, now. I won't hear it."

Stephanie signaled for a staffer and ordered two glasses of the hotel's best champagne. Missy couldn't help the snort of laughter that escaped.

"I understand we have something to 'almost' celebrate? James told me he nearly choked to death when George mentioned you 'tried' to give him a blow job!"

Steph did her best Teresa impression.

"Tried? Oh, puh-leez! That is *so* day before yesterday, dah-link!"

The champagne was served in the pool. Stephanie raised her flute to make a toast, her smile inscrutable. Missy raised hers in answer, positive she saw the devil dancing in her friend's eyes. She was right.

"Here's to blow jobs: The best marriage counselor in town!"

Eyes turned to stare at the two women crying with laughter and talking fellatio.

"Oh my god! Keep it down, Steph!"

Her friend was bubblier than the champagne. She looked every inch the cat that drank the proverbial cream.

Er...make that cum...

Chapter 49

Please don't worry, sir. Steph will walk me to the car and I'll drive straight home. I'll be there in twenty minutes, half an hour tops. Can't wait! Miss you tons! xxoo...

To say he was displeased was an understatement of epic proportion. Not with the text, mind you. Nor with Missy. James was fuming at himself.

Well, also at those clueless cockheads at Shindigo. The meeting started at eleven, an hour late. They'd been too busy indulging their number one priority: blowing Cuban cigar smoke up each others assholes. The business of actual business was of secondary concern. As such, it could, and did, wait.

James sighed. No wonder the company was in shambles. Happily, it was no longer his concern. He'd done his due diligence and seen the project through. Be that as it may, he didn't hold out a lot of hope for these overblown, out of touch clowns.

He'd checked his messages the second the meeting adjourned. As expected, there'd been a slew of them. A pulse began thrumming in his temple. He'd promised Missy to be back in time to take her to meet Stephanie and he'd failed. That it was beyond his control had no bearing on the end result.

With complete disregard for the pressing matters at hand, his mind snapped straight to Angeline. An image of her beautiful face etched itself into his cerebellum, every heartwrenching feature crystallized. Then, in the blink of an eye, she was gone. It was as though there'd been a temporary disconnect in his brain that was quickly repaired.

Yet, James was left with a strange sensation. A random shiver tingled down his spine.

Missy's last missive was in response to the slew of messages he'd fired off in apology. James saw no shame in saying he was sorry. In fact, just the opposite was true. To his way of thinking, real men apologized. The rest needed to find a pair.

Unclenching his jaw, he forced himself to relax. He changed into a faded pair of jeans and a tee. Scrunching the suit into a loose ball he did his best Beckham – drop-kicking it towards the hamper. Falling way short, he retrieved each piece and deposited them by hand. *Speaking of hands...*

James held his to his face and inhaled. *Nothing.* He tried again, knowing it was fruitless. As expected, still nothing. Missy's scent was long gone. Despite the disappointment, he grinned. After all, she would be home any minute. It was going to be his pleasure to...reapply.

He poured himself a cognac, allowing it little time to acclimate in his hand. Taking a hard pull, he chose a strategic spot in the front room. From his position on the curved Elizabethan sofa, he had a bird's eye view of the driveway, and as a natural extension, all incoming vehicles.

James glanced at his watch before settling back to await Missy's imminent arrival...

Chapter 50

Missy turned up the volume, bopping along to her favorite Toby Keith song. It was a straight shot home now, and she was giddy to get there. It was ridiculous, but being separated from James for even a few hours seemed endless.

Master...

The afternoon had turned out great, despite the shaky start. She'd laughed so hard her cheeks still hurt. Steph had been downright bawdy, a side she'd kept well hidden all these years. She'd given those gawking women something to talk about, that was for sure. It wasn't often you heard a refined, middle-aged female singing the praises of oral sex.

Missy took pride in knowing that she'd nudged her friend down the path of happily-ever-after. *Emphasis on 'down'.* She grinned. Perhaps she ought to write a how-to book on the sensitive subject. After all, James thought her writing skills – and her cocksucking skills—both pointed to a natural affinity.

Let's see now...

Outrageous titles popped into her head. *'The Happy Hummer'* and *'Sucking for Seniors'* both tickled her silly bone. And, while she was laughing like a loon, why not throw in a holiday edition or two? In her none-too-humble opinion, *'Let it Blow'* and *'He'll Never Passover Good Head'* were festive classics in the making. Of course, it wouldn't do to come across as cocky. A, er, swollen head was never attractive on a lady.

Missy wiped away a tear. She couldn't wait to share the hilarity with James. She envisioned his eyes crinkling with laughter as she straddled his lap and babbled on. Sometimes she loved the man so much it hurt. The messages he left while she was in the spa brought a lump to her throat and an ache to her heart.

There was no such thing as half-measures where James was concerned. His apology was direct and sincere. There were no ifs, no ands, and not a whiff of a but. He assumed full responsibility, promising to make up for the massage she'd forfeited with his own two hands. In turn, she promised to collect on his offer.

A sharp twinge low in her belly demanded her undivided attention. Missy held her breath until it passed, then exhaled with a groan. *How could I have forgotten?*

In her defense, the last time she'd found herself in swirling, chemically infused hot water was too many years ago to count. The stabbing pain was a vivid reminder that it hadn't ended well then, either.

Missy gnawed at her bottom lip. There was another risk factor besides bacteria. Sex. Hours upon hours of hot, animalistic sex. Her cheeks burned at the accuracy of the description. At the same time, her lips curled into a mischievous smile. The very thought of James made her wet.

Whore!

With two strikes against her, Missy still clung to a gossamer thread of hope. Maybe, just maybe, it was a random cramp, nothing whatsoever to worry about. When it struck the second time, she was forced to acknowledge the truth. This time the shooting pain was accompanied by an unmistakable burning sensation. She shoulder checked and pulled a U-y. There was a pharmacy less than a mile back. Cranberry juice would hold her over until morning, when she could call Dr. Chadwick.

With safety in mind, she drove past the murky parking lot at the back of the building. Instead, Missy parked on the side street and switched on her flashing lights. Deciding to leave her phone in the car, she gathered her purse and climbed out of the SUV. She'd only be a second.

The blow came out of nowhere, blindsiding her. She wasn't sure if she'd been knocked out, but somehow, she was on the ground and the world was fading in and out. From somewhere in the distance she heard a cackling laughter, oddly familiar. The hulk of a man bending over her had no face, just the most malevolent eyes she'd ever seen.

Missy opened her mouth to scream, but what emerged was an ineffectual squeak. It felt like a baseball was lodged in her throat and a siren was going off in her head. With every ounce of strength she possessed, she rolled onto her belly and clawed to get away.

She didn't get far.

He pinned her to the concrete with one giant boot to the small of her back. Her terror escalated to a level she never knew existed when the behemoth dropped to his knees beside her and pulled a loaded syringe from his pocket.

Missy fought like a wildcat, to no avail. He sank the hypodermic into her arm and scooped her up into his. She bounced like a rag doll as he jogged to a waiting vehicle. Her last conscious memory was of a vehicle door being opened from within.

A beige vehicle...

Chapter 51

Ethan couldn't remember ever being this excited. Well, maybe the day his mother's liver conked out. And, of course, any time he visited Mistress Nevaeh Starr.

But, other than that...

"Bobby, ya dumb fuck. Put your fucking seat belt on and stick to the fucking speed limit. Unless you've got a logical explanation as to why there's an unconscious female in the car? If not, maybe think about getting us to Montgomery Manor without attracting too much attention."

With her head lolling on his thigh, Ethan absently stroked her hair. Not with affection, mind you; he despised the trailer trash ingrate. No, he stroked her like a proud owner stroked any shiny new possession. He grinned at the analogy. *This* shiny new possession was going to wake up with one mother of a barbiturate hangover. No matter. Ethan preferred his possessions a little more beat up—pun intended. His grin widened.

He'd begun to wonder if she would ever venture out without that overprotective goody two-shoes hovering over her. The two of them made him more physically ill than gorging on carnival food and hopping on the roller coaster. The best you could hope for was to not get any on you.

Ethan didn't plan to get any on him. His was a foolproof scheme which included an absolutely brilliant exit strategy. Palms were greased on both sides of the law. His boys were well paid. His reputation remained impeccable. As it ought.

In short, every T was crossed, every i was dotted. Ethan Montgomery III left no stone unturned. He was bulletproof, more Teflon than Teflon itself. His squeaky clean record was proof. Ethan laughed so hard, Bobby was staring at him in the rear view.

"What the fuck you looking at?"

More than once over the past weeks the boys had insinuated that he should pack it in and get back to business as usual. He'd eavesdropped on conversations chock full of words like 'obsessed', and his personal favorite, *unhinged*. They contended that no bitch was worth the trouble, the return wasn't worth the risk. And that the boss was batty. Blah, blah, blah.

Like he'd waste a crap on what those morons thought.

Tucking Missy's errant locks behind her ear, his fingers touched on a goose egg so large, it would make Big Bird proud. It was the first time he attained anything close to a boner. His only regret was that he wasn't the one who'd inflict it.

Ah, well. Next time.

Ethan peeked down the neckline of her blouse, then helped himself to handful of untethered teat. Joggling it, he frowned. He far preferred the sweet, perky breasts of a juicy adolescent. These udders sagged like the cow that she was. He pinched an areola, *hard*. It would leave a deep, rainbow-colored bruise. He couldn't wait to see it. Flicking brutally at the nipple, his mind drifted.

The tricky part was done. It went off without a hitch, despite the dodgy location. His ingenius plan was at last coming to fruition, his Job-like patience finally rewarded. The rest would be easy, and very, *very* gratifying.

Her royal cuntness' chambers awaited her, replete with ropes, chains and handcuffs. She'd want for nothing, at least from his perspective, which was the only one that counted. There was even an extra special surprise waiting, custom designed just for her.

With that in mind, he fingered the silver chain shimmering at her throat. Snagging it with his forefinger, he tugged once. It gave him great satisfaction to roll down the window and toss it out into the night.

Ethan pulled her skirt up to her waist and shoved his hand between her deadweight legs. He mauled her crotch, wishing she were awake to appreciate his ministrations. He was disgusted to find her panties damp. The slut just couldn't wait to get home and get fucked. He doubted the two of them ever came up for air.

Oh, the delicious ways she would pay for her disrespect...

Chapter 52

"She could be *dead* in twenty-four hours, for Christ sake!"

James yearned to slam a receiver onto a cradle, but even that miniscule satisfaction was denied him. Instead, he jabbed the 'End Call' button so savagely, he almost dislocated his finger and disabled the phone at the same time.

This was all his fault! This was no rogue asthma attack. There was no equivocating.

Missy...

Frantic did not begin to describe his state. Bolts of electrified adrenaline swamped his nervous system in tsunami strength waves. He needed desperately to rock but there was nowhere to roll. Instead, he paced, willing himself to breath, forcing himself to focus.

Little one...

He'd known something was amiss long before it was substantiated as fact. One second he was lounging on the couch, sipping from a snifter of the finest cognac on the planet. The next, he was sitting bolt upright, the liquor turning sour on his tongue and bilious in his belly.

Baby...

He called her, leaving message after message. Knowing it was futile, he continued to press redial, nonetheless. He was grateful that Stephanie and George were on their way over, although Steph seemed in worse shape than him. If that were possible. She'd burst into tears when he called. There was terror in her voice when she confirmed that she'd walked Missy to the Volvo and waved goodbye as she'd driven away. She was unaware of any last minutes changes in plan.

"Oh, dear god, James. She told me she was going straight home."

Somehow, he'd managed to hold on. He'd fought back against the riptide of fear and dread, preserving his energy as critical seconds ticked by. Precisely thirty minutes past her expected arrival time, he'd dialed 911.

James had no intention of waiting twenty-four hours. He would find the persons responsible and he would hold them accountable. Either that, or he would die trying. He believed in soul-mates and eternal connections. Missy was his. They would live together or they would die together.

Missy...

James growled. Shaking his head, he swept the maudlin thoughts away. The time for self-pity was over. He could either continue to wallow or he could get his shit together and do what he used to do best: special reconnaissance.

During Desert Storm, he'd spent almost as much time behind enemy lines as the enemy. His point man? Bull Bobrov. Bull, aka Valerey, was a born and bred native of Brighton Beach, New York. At five foot nine and two hundred and forty pounds, nobody dared call him Valerey. Unless, of course, they were tired of living.

He and Bull were like brothers, blood brothers, in fact. He'd acted as Bull's crutch when he caught some shrapnel after a failed ambush. Bull had been like a dog with a bone, refusing to let it rest. As a result, James received a Bronze Star and Bull's eternal gratitude.

"Just tell me what ya need, bro."

James was back in the desserts of Kuwait. Every muscle fiber twitched in anticipation of action. Tunnel visioned, he focused on the mission and nothing but the mission. Bull was to check in on Luke before heading over. Although he was sure Luke wasn't directly involved, the possibility still needed to be eliminated.

There was no doubt who was behind this madness. In a strange way, the knowing gave him hope. That cocksucker Ethan had proven himself a patient man. Patient and insane. If his wish were simply to kill her, it would have been an uncomplicated matter. James was convinced his agenda lay elsewhere. Retribution. While it was a direction he dared not dwell upon, it was also a direction that would keep her alive.

For a time, at least.

Little one...

James, too, was a patient man. The difference? He wasn't bat-shit crazy. He refused to lose her, it was that simple. Angeline was bad enough. Missy would be too much. One thing was certain. Ethan Montgomery III would pay. James placed one last call. Officer Frank Shanahan didn't hesitate. He'd be over ASAP, the minute his shift ended.

James transformed his office into a military command center. This would be a precision-run operation. He, together with the three men joining him, brought a diverse spectrum of skills to the table. Every single one of them would be imperative to the success of this most vital mission.

Baby...

Failure was not an option.

Chapter 53

The images with the hood covering her face were his favorites. To be fair, it could be due to his acute loathing of the scag. Ethan scrolled through the photos again, as impartial as a judge. Still, the hood won out. Missy was definitely more attractive with it on than off.

Of course, Nevaeh Starr was the true artiste. He'd defer to her expert opinion, with pleasure. Ethan adjusted his stiffening dick. Just the thought of the cruel Dominatrix gave him a chubby. Her imminent arrival got his juices flowing. He sneered in Missy's direction. *She sure as fuck didn't.* Pre-cum oozed, soaking through his Calvin Klein's *and* his Valentinos.

Not long ago, a stain on his attire was as odious as a stain on his character. The hint of either was enough to hurl him into a tizzy. Yet, lately, such things seemed to matter less and less. He observed the expanding circle, and grinned.

He'd come to realize that there were but two things in life that mattered. Underage Asian hookers and Mistress Nevaeh Starr. Beating the crap out of baby hookers left him coming like a stallion on steroids. The same orgasmic results were achieved when Mistress beat the crap out of him.

To his way of thinking, it was quid pro quo, an exquisite symmetry of give and take. That one was consensual and one was not didn't enter into the skewed equation. When Ethan did the math, it worked out to his advantage every time. He consented on their behalf. After all, they *were* underage. He snickered. Next time, he'd make sure they thanked him.

Still unconscious, Missy looked right at home in her new habitat. Built with her discomfort in mind, the grimy mattress tossed onto the floor would no doubt illicit warm memories of her youth. He'd left her dressed, although her panties were pulled to one side and her hands were handcuffed over her head. Her ankles were chained as well, if only for aesthetic purposes. Perusing his impressive handiwork, Ethan was astonished.

How'd I ever get it up for...that?

Yet, there was no denying that he had. She'd milked him dry, playing him for a fool the entire time. He saw red every time he recalled the humiliation. Blood red. Somehow, her aggressive demeanor must have triggered subliminal fantasies of Nevaeh. The conniving cunt *had* manhandled him in her rush to satisfy her agenda. In answer, he'd performed like a well-trained baboon.

Ethan shook his head. He banished the vile memory, deleting the entire file from his mind and destroying the hard copy. His was the only agenda that counted, as she was about to find out. The bitch was right where she belonged: hooded, handcuffed and at his non-existent mercy. At last, the scales of justice were balanced. The planets were restored to alignment.

Well...almost.

He took more stills, from every angle, with and without the hood. He would wait until she was conscious, then switch to video. He would have his cake and make a tidy profit, too. There was a black market hungry for the type of footage he'd be filming over the next week.

Leaning over, he zoomed in to get an up-close-and-personal shot of her genitalia. Catching sight of his hand through the magnified lens, he paused, fascinated. His fingernails were a disaster. Not only were they filthy, they were ragged, bitten to the quick.

When did I start biting my nails again?

Muffled moans were coming from beneath the hood. Soon, the bitch was whimpering like a whipped dog. Ethan grinned at his choice of words. *If she only knew...*

His heart was pounding in his chest. She was coming to. He felt more alive than in his entire life. Seeing no reason to contain himself, he nearly bounced right out of his loafers. This was his magnum opus. It was time to raise the final curtain.

Snatching the hood from her head, he took a moment to bask in the glory of his accomplishment. Missy's eyes were slits against the sudden glare of spotlights. She was so pale, you'd think she'd seen a ghost. *Or Bobby.* Her hair was a bird's nest, a large chunk behind one ear matted with blood.

At last, her unfocused eyes settled on him. Her tongue clicked against a dry palate. Ethan assumed his most magnanimous smile.

"Good morning, sunshine! Welcome to Montgomery Manor. I'll be your host for the foreseeable future. Please, make yourself comfortable!"

Chapter 54

James sucked a turgid nipple into his mouth, teasing it with his lips, tongue, and – *oh, yes, please* – teeth. He didn't nibble, he consumed. The rumble of satisfaction from deep in his throat vibrated in her mind before manifesting itself as a river of desire between her legs. In the background, a clicking sound almost disrupted the perfection of the moment. Missy ignored it.

Arching her back in silent supplication, she offered herself to a noble Master. There was little wiggle room, what with her arms trussed above her head and her Master's full weigh atop her.

And...in her.

His cock was as rigid as reinforced steel. Buried to the hilt, his heartbeat pulsed against the welcoming walls of her sex. He filled her and he fulfilled her. His slightest pleasure was her greatest joy. His hand reached up to fasten around her collared throat, squeezing just enough to make her head spin. Relinquishing the nipple, he rose up to pierce her eyes with his.

"You are mine, little one. Never forget."

Missy inhaled him, oxygenating her lungs with his breath, nourishing her spirit with his words.

"I need you, my Master."

Her voice sounded guttural in her ears. The clicking in the background became more pronounced. Again, Missy ignored it, choosing instead to lose herself in her Master's eyes.

"Open your mouth, little one."

There was no logical explanation, but Missy knew what was coming. Obeying his directive, she extended her tongue in anticipation. When he spat upon it, she remained motionless, resisting the urge to savor it as one might the finest of wines. When his lips joined with hers, memories of their first kiss brought tears to her eyes. Between them, they feasted on his spittle and gorged on each other. Too soon, he tore his mouth from hers. Her eyes weren't the only ones filled with tears.

"I need you as well, my pet."

And with those words, James began to fade, his features dissolving into nothingness before her very eyes. His comforting weight lifted from her, leaving her shivering with cold. She begged him to stay, pleaded with him not to leave her. He couldn't hear her. Her voice was drowned out by that infernal clicking.

Maaasterrr...

There was nothing left to do but open her eyes. Reality struck like a blow to the back of the head.

Blackness.

Pain.

Terror!

All that remained of her sweet dream was that damned clicking noise. She was not in her Master's bed and whatever contraption was wrapped around her throat was not her Master's collar. A jackhammer played havoc with her skull. Against every instinct, Missy forced herself to remain still.

Where am I? How long have I been here?

It was so hard to focus. Shards of petrifying memories were scattered to the furthest corners of her consciousness. The last thing she remembered was being hit from behind and trying desperately to get away from a hulk of a man wearing a ski mask.

After that...nothing.

Her mouth felt like sandpaper, one breast throbbed. She assessed her physical condition, willing herself to not burst into tears. She took some small solace in the fact that she was clothed. Also, she'd somehow avoided a concussion, although pain radiated from the back of her head in crashing waves. Her low back ached, as well. While the gory details of how she'd wound up in this horrifying situation were hazy, the outcome was crystal clear.

Her wrists were handcuffed and her ankles were chained. Even more disconcerting was the bulky contraption around her neck. Its stiff nylon edges bit into her flesh. A large box in the front pressed against her larynx. Last, but far from least, some kind of leather bag was covering her head. From the opened bottom, she could just make out the lower portion of a pair of legs.

Men's.

Wing-tipped loafers.

Ethan!

Fragmented pieces of the puzzle snapped together in her mind. She recalled a booted foot holding her down and how desperately she'd fought to escape from under it. Fought and failed.

And then, there was the hypodermic needle. It floated in the blackness before her, as lethal looking as a machine gun. The memory of it aimed at her vein evoked a fear so intense, she pushed it back to the nether recesses of her subconscious. The beige hummer was the clincher. With that recollection, the last remnants of confusion were eradicated.

Her immediate concern was for the men in her life. Once again, she conjured James' face. This time, however, his brow was furrowed in distress. The thought of him worrying about her safety brought stinging tears to her eyes. They dripped down her face and into her ears. She was helpless to wipe them away. Swallowing hard, she reached out mentally to comfort the man she loved with her entire being.

Master...

Missy thanked god that Christopher was away at college. She prayed he would never need to hear of this. There was only one way for that to happen. She needed to get out of this, whatever *this* was.

Failure was not an option.

It would be a simple matter to choke on the balloon of emotion clogging her throat. Missy was overwhelmed, incredulous that Ethan could take a minor slight and contort it to this degree. Still, a single ray of hope shone through the suffocating wall of shock and dread. After all, she'd known Ethan for years.

While he'd always been eccentric, he was far from stupid. Even more ludicrous was the idea of the effeminate Ethan as a vicious hoodlum. He was the city's celebrated golden boy; feeder of the poor, supporter of the arts. Missy was sure she could reason with him.

With that decided, she moaned. Although the disembodied legs had moved out of her field of sight, the clicking continued. She moaned again. Somewhere inside, a dam broke. She began to moan and whimper in earnest, thrashing against the chains. She heard footfalls behind her, and then, blinding light.

With the hood removed, Missy squinted against the glare.

"Good morning, sunshine! Welcome to Montgomery Manor. I'll be your host for the foreseeable future. Please, make yourself comfortable!"

Missy followed his voice. Slowly, her eyes adjusted. Ethan was a mess. Unshaven, his hair was matted to his head and his clothing was rumpled. His contorted grin was made even more ghastly by its incongruity. Still, Missy was sure she could reasons with him. That is, until she looked into his eyes.

Empty.

Merciless.

Unhinged!

The words screaming in her head emerged as barely a croak. They scraped their way past her compressed larynx and cracked, dry lips.

"Oh, dear god. You've gone stark raving mad!"

Chapter 55

"Than' you, Mistress. May I please have...another?"

Missy was in a world of pain. She wasn't sure how much more she could endure. Her attempts at reason had fallen on deaf ears. Ethan had laughed at her, telling her she should have thought of the consequences before she'd humiliated him.

"Now, it's your turn."

She heard the hiss of the short whip a moment before it struck flesh. Her flesh. She braced instinctively, knowing it would do nothing to diminish the agony. Grunting with the impact, she gasped for air and salvation.

This was her second day as Ethan's prisoner and her second session with Mistress' whip. She'd heard the heartless harlot arguing with Ethan about having to use the shorter whip. She'd not been pleased. *After all, a long whip was so much more 'exciting', not to mention 'effective'.*

Missy was thankful for any small mercy at this point, if only a shorter whip. While it may not flay the flesh from her bones, she wouldn't wish this torture on anyone. Well...maybe one person. Unable to teleport herself into James' arms, she conjured his face to sustain her.

Her lip was split as was the skin along her right cheekbone. Ethan didn't bother to remove his rings before backhanding her. Her nose wasn't broken, but it was swollen. She literally could not see past it. If that weren't enough, her bladder burned. Missy cringed. Her damned plumbing was what got her into this mess in the first place.

The whip landed across her right shoulder, pouring gasoline onto a flame already ignited. For a moment, she couldn't breath.

"Than' you...Mithtress. May I...ha'...another..."

She never dreamed pain like this was possible. With childbirth, at least you knew what was coming. It was grueling, but expected. Visions of Christopher in her arms for the first time brought a different kind of tear to her eye. With childbirth, the reward nullified the pain, converting it instead into a badge of honor.

There were no rewards to be had in Ethan's house of horrors. Unless you counted the absence of punishment, which she did. At Montgomery Manor, the pain was just as much psychological as physical. Missy never knew what was coming, only that it was. And, when it did - it would be both humiliating *and* painful.

The shock collar was the worst. Barbaric. Depraved. Words didn't begin to describe the abomination. The very thought of it evoked a terror so profound, it left her breathless. Mindless. Hopeless.

And, this was no ordinary shock collar. Oh, no. This shock collar had been modified to Ethan's diabolical specifications. Proud as a peacock, he'd sung its praises, only too happy to explain the scope of its cruel attributes. He'd finished with a gut-churning warning.

"If you fuck with it, bitch, you'll be more than sorry. I had a special wire implanted, just for you. It runs full circle. If you break the connection, you'll be shocked non-stop until the battery in the remote dies."

Ethan shrugged.

"Or, until you do, whichever comes first."

Ethan was not reticent in testing his new toy, either. Her jaw ached from relentless clenching, every muscle throbbed from involuntary contraction. Her mind slurred, barely able to focus on the one thing that mattered. Survival. Once again, Ethan had been eager to share. He'd spoken with the bluster of a psychopath, his pupils dilated.

"Why do you think I bailed out your ex, slut? When you're found on his doorstep, one more parasite will be swept from the streets. Well...two, counting you."

His maniacal smile was almost as chilling as his maniacal words.

"Who's going to question it? Especially when one takes into account all the good folks in my back pocket and Luke's somewhat problematic track record where you're concerned. Tsk, tsk."

To Ethan's deranged mind, his scheme was foolproof. To Missy, that's all that mattered.

"James will find you and kill you."

She'd learned to shut the fuck up after that. Without warning, the internal mechanism in the shock collar was triggered. Hearing it, Missy had a split second to press her teeth together before the electrical current did it for her.

Her jaw locked. Every tendon in her throat distended to the point of intolerable agony, and then further. While the current was strongest at her throat and jaw, her extremities were not spared. They spasmed for the duration, contorted and useless.

There was no ability to think, only endure.

The terror that defined her existence indescribable. It was her constant companion, as malignant as a cancer. It undermined her determination, eroded her ability to concentrate. But, concentrate she must if she was to have any hope of escape.

"Hank you, Mistress...please...plea...another..."

Missy was nude, wrists and ankles locked into 'stocks' that were, in turn, bolted to the inside of the door frame. Her legs were spread, arms stretched overhead. Ethan stood before her, camera in one hand, remote control in the other. He couldn't wait to punish her if she were reticent in thanking Mistress for the last lash or begging for the next.

As hideous as it was, she'd take a whipping over the shock collar any day. The two combined were so excruciating, Missy feared she wouldn't survive the ordeal. Breathless and twitching, she nonetheless made sure to thank Mistress for every stroke. And, to beg her for the next.

"Haan ou..Mithess...nother...pleas..."

Chapter 56

Missy was right where she belonged: beneath him. Deep within her, he held her ever-so-close. Still, she trembled in his arms. James brushed her quivering lips with his. Tasting salt, he kissed the moisture from her cheeks before burying his face in her hair and weeping silent tears of his own.

"I need you, my Master."

"I need you as well, my pet."

Yet, with those words, Missy began to fade, her features dissolving into nothingness before his very eyes. Without her, James was bereft, left frantic with cold desperation. He called out, scrambling to reach her before she was gone.

"You are mine little one. Never forget!"

Her lips moved in response, barely there. He strained to make out the words, but couldn't. And, then, she just...disappeared.

Little one...

There was nothing left to do but open his eyes. It Reality struck like a siren straight to the cerebellum.

No! That was the phone!

James leaped from the sofa in his office, alert, every muscle coiled and ready for battle. This was Missy's third day missing, the thirty-fifth hour. He'd gotten six hours sleep in that time, and only to appease Stephanie.

The Volvo was located the first day, illegally parked on a side street next to a pharmacy. Not two miles from home, the flashers were on, her phone inside. It was obvious she'd stopped to pick something up at the last minute. She'd never made it into the store.

Frank Shanahan made sure he was assigned to the investigation, and apprised James every step of the way. They were few gainful steps to boast of. The only clues found at the scene were a syringe cap and a small amount of blood on the concrete.

Dread congealed in the pit of his stomach, using guilt as its glue. He would not—*could not*—allow himself to think about what she must be suffering. It would paralyze him, rendering him useless. His singular focus must remain on finding Missy. Alive. Today. Everything else they could deal with later. Together. With Herculean will power, he dumped the disabling emotions into a mental crate, sealed it, and stored it for future agonization.

Bull had a list of Ethan's known addresses before the police were even on point. There were three in the city: two penthouse residences and one office suite. It was no surprise to anyone that Ethan preferred looking down on the rest of the world.

Detectives paid each high-profile building a visit, with dismal results. Buzzers were pressed, doormen were questioned, cards were left. Nothing, nothing, and more nothing. There wasn't enough, or, *any* evidence to even secure search warrants.

Gutted, James nonetheless understood that search warrants would be a colossal waste of time, time they didn't have. All three buildings had security up the yin-yang. All were monitored on-site 24/7/365. It would be close to impossible for a drugged, bleeding woman to slip by unnoticed.

Where did that son of a bitch take her?

In his heart, James knew she was alive. He *felt* it, felt *her*. The question that kept the adrenaline pumping and his mind racing was: *for how long?*

"Hello?"

The second James picked up the phone, George Weatherly came careening into the office, waving a document in the air. He'd been scouring Ethan's juvenile cases. *Was that excitement in his eyes?*

Wondering why George was lit up like a Christmas tree, James pointed to the phone at his ear and held up a finger. He turned back to the call, listening without interruption.

Hanging up, he beamed back at George. Now, they were both excited. The two old friends spoke as one.

"I know where she is!"

Chapter 57

"That high falutin boy never did have no respect. Not for no one, most 'specially womenfolk. I seen the devil's work in him from a way back. He know I know it, too. I'm sorry to say, but, this dirty business don't surprise me none."

After Frank Shanahan's call, they'd raced to the rural address of the Montgomery's long time maid. Emphasis on raced. The authorities, who were subject to sluggish red tape and exacting procedure, were at least an hour behind. That was just fine with James.

The trio looked like a group of homeless hooligans who didn't own a razor blade between them. Wedged shoulder to shoulder with George and Bull, James was antsy, claustrophobic. There was as much adrenaline in his veins as there was hemoglobin. He needed to harness it until the time was right.

Little one...

Birdie Washington cut an impressive figure. Black as ebony, her skull-tight afro was a shocking white in contrast. Eighty years old, she had a sturdy build, if compact. She was maybe four-foot-ten, four-foot-eleven, tops. She sat in her shabby chair at her shabby kitchen table with her spine arrow straight and her head held high. James took an immediate liking to the scrappy old woman.

"I done tried to tell folks a way back. Made a po-lice report and all. Cheeky chile, callin' me 'Mammy', and worse. Just like he done when I gone over to the big house this mornin'."

Her voice was strong, her mind sharp as a tack. Her story held every man in the room spellbound.

"Ya see, I been away, visitin' my ailin' sister. She got the cancer, like Mr. Montgomery got the cancer. When I get back, this note's on the door."

The note was signed Master E. Montgomery III: *Montgomery Manor is being prepared for sale. Your services will not be required for the entire week.*

"I knows the big house ain't for no sale. I visit Mr. Montgomery two times every month, more if the arthritis ain't hurtin' too bad. Mr. Montgomery says that boy can't never sell that house out from under him. It's in writin', he says."

"So, I go see with my own eyes what he be up to. He don' know it, but there's an old path cuts straight through them trees. He took his time bout gettin' to the door, too. I ask him what the nonsense bout sellin' Mr. Montgomery's house."

Birdie Washington's arthritic hand reached for the glass of water in front of her. James could tell the small movement caused her great pain. His respect for the indomitable woman grew deeper. She took a few small sips while James forced himself to breath.

"Right away, I see somethin's off bout him. He's dirty, like he ain't washed. That ain't right, that boy's a prissy one. He won't let me in neither, just cracks the door is all. Told me to get my nigger ass home and mind my own f'n business."

She looked around her miniscule, sparkling clean kitchen, making eye contact with each of the three men. If she felt outrage within, the pride in her eyes belied it. James imagined she'd seen and heard worse in her eighty years. He hung his head, overcome with empathy and sick with shame. Birdie picked up where she'd left off, her voice now fortified with iron.

"When I was walkin' away, I seen her. Up on the second floor, in his old room. The good lord hisself made me turn back around, only reason I kin think of. She was there, then she was gone – like black magic. But, I seen her, don't be doubtin' ole Birdie. A she-devil, I tell you. Big as Goliath. Bigger.

"Imagine these old bones runnin'. I come straight home to call the po-lice..."

James looked out Birdie Washington's kitchen window. Off-duty, Officer Shanahan was just coming up the gravel drive. James turned back to the old woman. Taking her deformed hands gently into his, he kissed the gnarled back of each. Words escaped him. One last kiss to her cheek and he was out the door.

The woman he loved was just beyond that grove of trees. Ethan Montgomery was living on borrowed time...

Chapter 58

Missy had a plan. Now, all she needed was the opportunity – and the courage, to implement it. Today was the third day of her incarceration. It was also the day she'd overheard that there wasn't to be a fourth. An unexpected visitor had pushed Ethan into a rabid frenzy. It wouldn't surprise her if he were frothing at the mouth.

Somewhere in the bowels of the house, heavy objects were crashing against walls. Chained and cowering on the disease infested mattress, Missy listened as he ranted at the top of his lungs.

I should have fucking known! That meddling nigger never could follow a simple order. This place has to be cleaned out and the loose ends tied up—NOW!

Missy knew that she was the 'loose end' of which he spoke. Her blistered throat closed. The faces of James and Christopher materialized in her mind, beckoning for her to join them. She gathered what was was left of her meager strength. This was one loose end that wasn't about to be 'tied up' without a fight.

Master...

It was now or never.

In an ironic twist of fate, it was Ethan's enthusiasm for the shock collar that exposed a possible avenue for escape. Yes, he very much enjoyed his little toy, using it for any infraction, imagined or real. When he was in the room, she was never chained. The sick bastard derived far more pleasure watching her contort at the press of a button.

She'd been introduced to the abhorrent device the first day. He'd unchained her, then demonstrated level one. Or, as he called it: *A little taste of what would happen if she tried to run.* Missy did not try to run. Level one was more than enough to scare the living shit out of her.

The next time was mere minutes later when she'd refused to take off her clothes.

"Fuck you, Ethan!"

He'd stood above her, wild-eyed with fury, the dreaded remote control in his hand. For a moment, she thought he might use it to strike her, but, that was not the case. Instead, he kicked it up a notch to level two, backhanding her across the face for good measure.

Ethan wasn't a fan of the hood, using it exclusively when Mistress was present. For his part, he preferred to see the pain and fear in her eyes. It was the only way he got off. She'd come to realize that the afternoon on her couch was an anomaly. Be that as it may, level two was a sharp upswing in intensity from level one. She was left twerking like a rag doll in its wake, brain waves flat-lined.

The second she regained control of her muscles and her mind, Missy took off her clothes—every last stitch. Tears streamed down her face as her trembling fingers all but ripped them from her body. Ethan recorded the entire horrific scene, laughing like the lunatic he was.

Mistress arrived the first night, although she didn't 'introduce' herself until the following morning. For the duration, Missy was hooded, blindfolded, or both. She was not provided a name beyond Mistress. Instead, the introduction included her first visit to the stocks, her first whipping - and her face being mounted!

Sight unseen, Missy knew who the heartless harlot was. The malevolence she exuded bore a singular signature. She remembered her first impression back at Hillside Golf and Country Club. A chill as cold as ice had run down her spine. *A premonition?* That dreadful whip tattoo on her arm now made perfect sense.

There was no mistaking those muscular thighs, especially when they were squeezing Missy's head like a stubborn pimple. She partook of what lay between them with the enthusiasm of a child licking her favorite ice cream cone.

Of course, that was after Ethan zapped her with a level three electrical shock.

And, after she'd discovered that level three? *Didn't work!*

She'd braced for it, convinced she was about to die. She'd whined and whimpered for mercy, to no avail. When the mechanism in the collar triggered, all she could do was set her teeth, squeeze her eyes, and pray to God.

Nothing?

Missy thought faster than a bolt of lightning. Simulating effects she was far too familiar with, she threw herself backwards. She locked her joints, violently hyper-extending her back until only her head and flopping heels touched the mattress. A high-pitched wail hissed from her brutalized throat, lasting until the mechanism stopped buzzing. For good measure, her bladder loosed. Missy collapsed atop the mattress, jerking and shuddering in feigned aftershock.

When Mistress climbed aboard the second time, Missy didn't hesitate. She feasted on pussy and planned her escape...

Chapter 59

It was now or never...

There was as much adrenaline in her veins as there was hemoglobin. She needed to harness it until the time was right.

Cursing under his breath, Ethan was stomping up the sweeping, curved staircase. Straight out of *Gone With The Wind*, it was the same sweeping, curved staircase Missy would need to descend if she were to have any hope of escape.

Unconscious when they'd arrived, she'd had no idea what lay outside the four damask walls of her prison. That is, until she'd been bound into the open doorway for her first flogging. With Mistress wielding the whip at her back, Ethan removed the hood to derive his own twisted pleasure.

Abused and tormented by both, she'd lost all hope. But, unbeknownst to her at the time, she'd gained something, as well. Insight. Or, in this case, *out*-sight: a panoramic view of what lay beyond. There was no egress within her line of vision. However, she did spy an ornately-tiled corner of what appeared to be a foyer.

Not that it mattered. *At the time.*

Now, it meant the difference between life and death. If the opportunity for escape presented, that foyer was her first objective. Her second? *Getting the fuck out of this torture-chamber!* All she could do was pray that a door appeared to expedite the process.

She needed to get a minimum of twenty-five feet away from that remote control and a world away from Ethan Montgomery III. Geographically speaking, she had no idea where she was. There was no sound of traffic and the nights were black as pitch. There had to be somebody in close proximity that could help her. She was in no shape to be running a marathon.

Missy worried her torn lip. There were so many factors to consider and she couldn't possibly be thinking straight. She'd had nothing to eat or drink in days, other than watery gruel and milky water. Served in crystal bowls and tossed onto the revolting mattress, cutlery was not provided. With one zap, she'd learned that using her hands was also forbidden.

She'd resisted for a time, until, eventually, she'd crammed her face into the bowls and licked them both clean. While the vile contents proved minimal sustenance, it was better than nothing. Perpetually lightheaded and terrified, her ability to concentrate was poor at best. Add to that a cruel regimen of beatings and shock treatments, and Missy's coordination was also sorely lacking.

Her willpower, however, was not. In her delirium, she felt James' presence. His arms enveloped her, a blanket of strength and courage. She'd swear she caught a trace of his scent. Missy cinched her aching shoulders back. She might only have one shot at escape, but she was determined to make it count despite the odds.

Master...

It all came down to this. If Ethan punished her with anything other than a level three jolt; she was a dead woman.

If he selected the correct intensity, her plan was simple: *RUN LIKE HELL!*

Her job now was to make sure the lunatic got it right. A treacherous undertaking in and of itself, it was her only hope. There was nothing stopping him from just pulling out a gun and shooting her in the head. She vibrated with terror, refusing to dwell.

There was as much adrenaline in her veins as there was hemoglobin. She needed to harness it until the time was right. Missy forced herself to breath.

Ethan unchained her.

"Get up, bitch."

Missy stared straight ahead, doing her best imitation of broken. It wasn't a stretch. Ethan was distracted, more manic than ever. Unable to stand still, he paced the room, dessimating what was left of his cuticles. Used to instantaneous compliance, it took him a few seconds to realize that she hadn't. He stopped pacing.

"What the fuck is wrong with you? I said get up!"

Instead, she curled into a ball. What she hoped looked like demoralized withdrawal was in fact, coiled conviction. Every muscle in her body was on high alert, ready to bolt at a moment's notice.

Ethan didn't know what to make of it, so he did what came naturally. He lashed out with his free hand, slapping her hard across the face. Missy barely flinched. In her mind, she was already out the door. She lifted her eyes to meet his, enunciating each word.

"Fuck you."

Stunned, Ethan froze. As did time. From somewhere outside her body, she watched herself face-off with a madman.

"It's over, you crazy ass motherfucker! Can't you hear the sirens?"

Of course, there were no sirens. Missy's gut piped up, so loud it overrode the ringing in her ears. Every instinct screamed for her to run. She obeyed. In an abrupt change of plan, she bolted for the opened door. She couldn't take the risk of being zapped with level two. She'd be incapacitated, completely out of options.

This was the only way.

The mechanism triggered just as she reached the top of the stairs. She braced, panic overcoming her. Thanks to forty hours of brutal conditioning, she set her jaw as her legs turned to rubber.

Nothing!

She flew. Half way down the stairs she saw the door. Three-quarters of the way down, she heard Ethan behind her. The mechanism buzzed again and again. Missy wrenched at the door like a madwoman. It didn't budge. He was half-way down, dangerously close to the twenty-five foot safety zone.

In her mad panic, she'd neglected to throw the dead bolt. It took two attempts before her trembling fingers could manage the task.

The collar triggered just as Missy ran from the house, screaming as loud as her injured vocal chords would allow.

Maaasterrr...

Chapter 60

They used the pathway through the woods, if you could call it that. Obstacle course was a more fitting description. How an arthritic, eighty-year-old woman managed to negotiate it was beyond James. Even for two strong men, the going was slow and arduous.

Overgrown from years of disuse, James swiped at branches, holding them out of the way for Bull to pass. Stumps and uprooted trees littered the winding trail. Some they climbed over, others required a time consuming detour. At last, they emerged behind an outbuilding on the west side of the estate.

It took every ounce of self-control he possessed to not simply storm the overblown symbol of pompous gluttony. They'd gotten a late start, thanks to a disagreement with Frank Shanahan regarding tactics. Frank insisted the best plan of attack was to sit tight and wait for backup to arrive. James vehemently disagreed.

Little one...

He wasn't about to sit with his thumb up his ass hoping the cops arrived before Ethan decided to do something more...permanent. Birdie's unscheduled visit was sure to have sent him into a tailspin, if not a full-blown meltdown. He'd gone to great lengths to ensure his sick plot was carried out in secrecy. Now, he knew his cover was blown. Every second counted.

In the end, he'd put his hand on his friend's shoulder and looked him in the eye.

"Go home, Frank. You were never here. I won't allow you to jeopardize your career. As it is, I'll never be able to repay you for everything you've done."

Their eyes remained locked until, at last, Frank blinked. The two men hugged, friends for life. James waited until his cruiser was out of sight, then he and Bull made a beeline for the trees.

Emerging on the other side, James estimated that they were now a scant ten minutes ahead of the law. Still, it was enough time for his purposes. He was so close to Missy, he'd swear he could smell her. He reached out with his heart and his mind, wrapping his arms around her.

I'm coming, little one.

They'd just found an unlocked patio door when there was a loud commotion around front. It sounded like a door slamming. Or...crashing open. And, there was something else...

James bolted, going from zero to sixty in the blink of an eye. Tears streamed down his face as he screamed, howled, bellowed her name. He tore across the manicured lawns at full throttle, arms and legs pistoning.

"Baby! I'm coming! I'm right here! Oh, my god! Jesus fucking Christ! This way, little one! *RUN!*"

James instantly recognized the shock collar for what it was. Vomit and rage welled up in his throat. He managed to quell the one while giving free rein to the other. Missy's face was contorted, a mask of terror. Her mouth was open in mid-scream, yet only a croak emerged.

Behind her, Ethan careened from the gaping doorway. Missy collapsed halfway between them. Without missing a beat, James made a minute alteration in direction and kicked it into overdrive. He tackled the cocksucker at the knees, knocking him backwards into the doorway.

"Bull! Get George to bring the car. Get her the fuck out of here!"

The two men grappled their way further into the house. They were about the same size, but where James was fit, his opponent was flaccid. Not to mention cowardly. Begging for mercy in a falsetto whimper, Ethan's eyes were squeezed shut. He thrashed wildly, catching James in the mouth with the hard plastic corner of the remote control.

James felt no pain. An overdose of adrenalin and a gut load of rage made sure of that. He did, however, feel his lip split open and a gush of hot blood spurt from the wound. He snarled, wresting the heinous object from Ethan's grasp.

He could just make out the distant wail of sirens as he kicked the door shut behind him.

Chapter 61

James sat at her bedside, his bandaged hands engulfing hers. His lips were stretched from ear-to-ear in a suture splitting grin.

To Missy, the private room looked more like the Taj Mahal than a hospital. It came equipped with a mini-fridge, four-piece private bath, recessed lighting – even a dimmer switch. His extravagance was as touching as it was unnecessary. She'd be just as content in a dank, dark cave. The only creature comfort she needed at that moment was sitting right beside her, his smiling eyes gazing into hers. Everything else fell away as insignificant.

Master...

The hospital staff was wonderful. Her wounds were attended to, a salve for her back and throat, stitches to her cheekbone and lip. While her voice was a raspy croak for now, the doctors were optimistic for its full recovery. James was there every step of the way, his beloved face a paradox of emotion. Worry was etched into his brow, while pure joy shone from his eyes.

For her part, she couldn't take her eyes off him. He was her oasis after a long, dry trek in the desert.

Master...

A second bed was wheeled into the room for James. He'd made it clear he was here for the duration. It was hard not to notice the nurses twittering around him, eager to see to his comfort. An observer might wonder who was the actual patient. Like planets to the sun, they orbited, his aura gravitational. Missy smiled, noting that most of their eyes were cast down. She wasn't surprised.

James glanced over at the cot. Lifting one eyebrow, he glanced away, dismissing it out of hand. It was obvious he felt a second bed redundant, a waste of time and space. Wild horses would be hard-pressed to drag him from her side.

He insisted on blaming himself. She refused to hear such nonsense. Likewise, he wouldn't allow her to assume even a smidgen of responsibility. They made a pact right then and there. From that day forth, all blame would be laid where it belonged: squarely on the shoulders of Ethan Montgomery III. With that settled, years of soul-sucking guilt were nullified.

Just as the deal was struck, a technician arrived to take Missy away. She underwent a slew of tests including X-rays, blood work, neurological and gynecological exams. She even completed a rape evidence kit, despite insisting she wasn't raped. The doctor, bless her patient heart, treated her like a reticent five-year-old.

"Yes, dear. Of course not, dear. This is just a precaution, dear."

Getting the shock collar off had been the worst. Ethan had been only too happy to hand over the key after his short 'tete-a-tete' with James. Yet, when the paramedics approached her with it in the ambulance, Missy shook so hard she must have registered on the Richter scale. Without a word, James had held out his hand, and was given the honor.

Once free of the barbaric accessory, she'd collapsed against him, sobbing with relief. He'd cradled her, murmuring words of love and empowerment against her clammy skin. There could be no better medicine. He was the perfect antidote. Soon, her sobs were downgraded to sniffles and hiccups.

"I'm so proud of you, little one. You are so brave, so clever, so resilient. Thank you for coming back to me."

Their lips had come together then, as they were meant to do. It proved an excruciating misstep. Hers were torn, bruised—swollen to twice their normal size. James' hadn't fared much better. Blood still leaked from the stitches. With matching lacerations, kissing would be off the table for the foreseeable future.

How she'd managed to chuckle at that juncture was beyond her. In any case, she'd taken it as a very good sign.

"Awww...we're going to have matching scars, sir."

She returned to her room to find George and Stephanie. From behind a massive bouquet of flowers stepped a beaming Teresa. Also there was a team of police investigators. While she welcomed her friends and climbed back into bed, they busied themselves questioning James.

They were wondering about the extent of Ethan's injuries, and how they might have been incurred. Aside from multiple scrapes and bruises, he'd somehow sustained a broken nose, a sprained wrist, and three broken ribs.

Ethan was of no use to them. Unresponsive, he was currently curled up in the fetal position with his back to a seething, murderous skinhead; aka his new cellmate. His verbal skills seemed limited to moaning and whimpering, with the occasional shrill cackle thrown in for good measure.

As the poker-faced police detective so eloquently put it, "Mr. Montgomery is unavailable for questioning at the moment."

It may be wrong, but it took every ounce of restraint for Missy not to grin. The way she saw it, 'Mr. Montgomery' was getting off easy. She'd lock that shock collar around his neck and have a heyday.

A shiver ran up her spine. The very thought of the despicable device invoked already conditioned responses. Her jaw locked. Her tongue sought refuge from her gnashing teeth. The physical scars would heal. Nevertheless, it was a mind bending ordeal she'd never forget. It seemed surreal that it ended just a few short hours before.

Police and ambulances had arrived en mass to Montgomery Manor, sirens blaring. She'd been sitting in the back of George Weatherly's car with George and James' old army buddy, Bull. James, however, had not yet emerged from the house.

Master...

If Missy had been afraid for herself, she'd been petrified for James. When that door closed, she was convinced she'd never see him again. To her, Ethan was the archetype of pure evil; the devil incarnate. Inconsolable, the gentle giant wrapped his jacket around her naked, convulsing form and begged her not to worry.

"I've known your man a long time, miss. I can promise you have nothing to fear."

His shy earnestness earned him a place in her heart forevermore.

Now, safe and sound at her Master's side, she listened as James filled in the blanks for the inquiring detectives.

"He was going for Missy. If he got within range, he could have killed her. There was no choice but to try to restrain him. Unfortunately, he resisted, ran back into the

KL SILVER

house, then managed to fall down that ridiculous staircase. That's when your boys arrived."

James' face was angelic, guileless.

"That's it in a nutshell, Detectives. Other than what Missy's told me, that's all I saw with my own eyes."

Chapter 62

Well...may not quite all.

James would never forget standing in the open doorway of Missy's makeshift prison. It was impossible to tell which was louder: his heart hammering in his ears or the cacophony of sirens outside the front door. Both were deafening. Yet, through it all, he could still make out Ethan's semi-conscious moaning. It was the only bright spot in James' very black mood.

It was coming from the bottom of the stairs where he'd left him. Ethan hadn't fallen. Every last one of his injuries was inflicted by hand. *James' hand!*

Looking into the shit hole where he'd kept Missy chained like an animal, James reconsidered his hard-fought decision not to kill him. The idea of the woman he loved being subjected to these conditions made him physically ill. Known to have a cast iron constitution, his stomach heaved. The pain and terror she experienced was an almost tactile presence. Not only could he smell it, he could feel it.

Little one...

Arm and leg irons were welded into the doorway in which he stood. *Jesus Christ, are those stocks?* A bare mattress in the corner was urine, blood, and feces stained. Beside it sat a bucket, half-filled with human waste. There were leather straps hanging from beams in the ceiling. A gynecological table, complete with stirrups, was piled high with unspeakable atrocities.

Outside, the police were putting the finishing touches on their plan of attack. Any second, they'd storm the house to discover the aftermath of his fury. By way of a megaphone, they beseeched Ethan to release his hostage. *Hostage?* James' brain was slow to make sense of it.

He needed to pass on the intel that would allow them to stand down. Instead, James found himself at the examination table, his legs having a mind of their own. He swiped at his eyes to clear his vision. His hand trembled as he picked up a whip. Touching it, a white hot rage coursed through his veins. The initials M.N.S. were burned into the braided leather shaft.

M.N.S.? *Who the fuck is M.N.S?* James had already determined the house empty, other than himself and the sniveling heir apparent begging for help on the floor below. Clearly, he'd had at least one accomplice. One who knew their way around a whip and was cold-hearted enough to use it on an innocent girl.

James was helpless against the all-consuming urge to wrap the whip around Ethan's throat. He would pull just hard enough to extract a name, and then just a wee bit harder. He turned with that precise goal in mind when the front door burst open. The clatter of boots and shouting of orders ensued. As did Ethan's weeping.

About to join the ruckus downstairs, a glint caught his eye. On a stool to the left of the doorway was a high-tech digital camera with video capability. James froze. He'd swear the blood in his veins turned to ice. In what seemed like slow motion, he picked it up. He had a split second to make a decision.

Decision made, James descended the vulgar staircase, tears flowing. Without a word, he handed the camera to the first officer he saw and continued out the door. He saw no good reason to have those images stamped into his mind. It was bad enough that Missy would have to wrestle with them for the rest of her life.

As he made his way to the ambulance where she anxiously awaited, he felt his heart swell near to bursting. His throat closed, but not before his eyes filled. In that moment, James swore to make it his life's mission to eradicate those gruesome images from her mind.

Little one...

Missy confirmed James' suspicions of a cohort. Her voice trembled as she described the whip-wielding dominatrix she knew only as Mistress. She swore she'd heard the two arguing not long before she'd escaped. Yet, a thorough and detailed search of the massive estate and its grounds didn't unearth a single soul. It would seem the femme fatale simply vanished into thin air.

Mistress? *That took care of the 'M'...*

An unmarked, tan colored, first edition Hummer with blacked out windows was swarmed as it turned onto Montgomery Drive. Bobby, the driver, was arrested, read his rights, and taken into custody. The muscle-bound Neanderthal feigned ignorance and innocence. He swore up and down that he was just the chauffeur, coming to pick up the boss.

In the chauffeur's pocket, they found a used syringe. In plain view on the passenger seat was an arsenal of evidence. It included rolls of duct tape, restraints, and a stun gun.

Last but not least was a Beretta semi-automatic pistol, complete with silencer...

Chapter 63

"I want to fuck you in France, spank you in Sicily, and pamper you in Portugal."

The lights were dimmed. At last, they were alone, swollen face to swollen face. The soft bleep of hospital monitors played in the background. Just outside the door in the bustling hallway, doctors were being paged and emergency codes were being called. To Missy, it was all just background music to a love song. *Her* love song.

Master...

Snug in her narrow hospital bed, their feet intertwined as they were wont to do. Each basked in the miraculous presence of the other, both ever-so-grateful for the opportunity. Gently, James stroked her bruised and bloated face. He told her again and again that she was beautiful. He spoke of the wrinkles and scars of life, and how they could never detract from her essence.

"To me pet, you are beauty personified. It radiates from the inside out, a reflection of your very soul. That will never change."

She hung on his every word. In her mind, they were etched in granite and underlined with blood. Lost in the lilt of his voice, the heat of his hands, and the beat of his heart, she felt herself healing. Also from the inside out. James was her Master, her one true love. She would worship him with her last breath. Missy shivered, well aware of how close she'd come.

"I miss my collar, sir."

James cupped her face, rubbing her nose with his, Eskimo style. He was silent, but Missy read the unspoken question in his eyes. And the anguish. She repeated the words, her voice a ragged croak.

"I want my collar."

She watched as a glut of emotion rearranged his features, one of which was sweet relief. The anguish remained, but it was dissipated. He was beginning to believe she might survive with her spirit intact. So was she.

"And, you shall have it, little one. As soon as you are healed. Trust me."

She did, there was no question of that. Missy couldn't take her eyes from him, afraid that if she did, she'd wake up to find it was all a dream. She prayed such things only happened on television. The corners of his blood-crusted lips lifted into a grin. His eyes shone.

"I want to adore you in Aruba, manhandle you in Martinique, and of course, Dominate you in the Dominican."

Missy giggled, snuggling as close as she could without ripping out the IV. If the nurses had liked James earlier, they adored him now. Other than monitoring her vital signs or changing the saline bag on the IV stand, James had taken over most of their duties.

He changed her dressings, careful to adhere to their detailed instructions. He gave her a sponge bath, perhaps paying a tad more attention to her breasts than hospital policy might advocate. When he washed her hair, the feeling of his strong fingers massaging her scalp was indescribable. Slow, silent tears streamed down her face for the duration.

When required, he also helped her to the washroom. However, James didn't feel it prudent to close the door. With an almost straight face, he explained that it was a safety precaution, nothing more.

Master...

He was still smiling at her when his eyelids began to droop. He was exhausted and with good reason. For her part, she was still on 'vibe'. Missy knew that when she crashed, it was gonna be a doozie. In the meantime, James helped her to roll over, holding the IV line out of her way. With her back to him, he pulled her bottom tight against him, spoon style.

As was his ritual, one arm encircled her waist, holding her close. The other supported her head, his hand reaching around to gently cup her breast.

James buried his face in the hollow between her shoulder and neck. Kissing his way up to her ear, he tongued it inside and out, and...stopped? *That's odd.* His hand was squeezing, no—kneading her breast. She wriggled her rump against him.

"I'm guessing you're not as tired as you look, sir?"

She was teasing, of course. Until she felt the hot tears in her hair.

"Sir?"

Silence. Missy was just about to burst into tears of her own when he spoke. They were the last words in the world she expected to hear.

"If it's a girl, I want her to look just like you."

Was he dreaming? She'd heard the words, but her brain was unable to interpret their meaning. It was as if they were spoken in another language, from another planet. Yet, for some reason, she started to cry. She might be slow, but she wasn't stupid.

"Oh my god! You think I'm pregnant? But...how?"

Could there be a stupider question? Missy might be facing away from him, but she knew he was grinning like the Cheshire Cat. His lips were pressed against the nape of her neck, just above the dressing.

Was it possible? Missy began to count days. When she ran out of her own fingers and toes, she borrowed James'. It wasn't until she reached the first digit of his fourth extremity that she stopped.

It *was* possible. But...not probable. After all, she would know. Wouldn't she? She'd known early enough with Christopher. True or not, the idea thrilled her. She knew how much James regretted not having children. And, she'd always wanted a girl.

He pulled his arm from beneath her and used it to prop himself up. He smiled down at her.

"Time will tell, my pet. In the meantime, I want to molest you in Mexico and eat you in Italy. Last but not least, I want to marry you in Maui. Will you have me, little one?"

The love beaming from his eyes was so bright, she was spellbound. The last few days had changed nothing. Missy felt weightless, breathless with joy.

"Oh, yes. Yes, my Master."

If their lips were unable to touch, there were no such constraints on their hearts and souls. Once again, Master and whore found themselves deep within the other—trussed for all eternity...

About the Author

K.L. SILVER writes romantic erotica novels and XXX novellas.

She adds a psychological edge which keeps YOU, the reader, on the edge of your seat. Or, such is the plan.

If that fails, there's a backup plan: A *lot* of hot S-E-X!

Now, where were we? Oh yes...

K.L. grew up, and still lives on the frozen prairies of central Canada. She lives alone, because she can. Her children have grown up to become strong, independent, and most exciting of all—gainfully employed adults. (YES!)

K.L.'s crazy enough to believe yoga and instant coffee keep her sane. Her primary goal is to write a great story. Her second, of course, is world peace.

Namaste

* * * * *

If you enjoyed TRUSSED, please do the author the honor of leaving a short review. Reviews are an indie author's life blood.

If you missed the prequel to TRUSSED – Get MASTERED today!

(viewBook.at/GETMASTERED)

SPANK you xx(X)